RICE
WITHOUT
RAIN

RICE
WITHOUT
RAIN

BY MINFONG HO

LOTHROP, LEE & SHEPARD BOOKS
NEW YORK

9   10

Library of Congress Cataloging in Publication Data
Ho, Minfong. Rice without rain.
Summary: After social rebels convince the headman of a small village in northern
Thailand to resist the land rent, his seventeen-year-old daughter Jinda finds herself
caught up in the student uprising in Bangkok. 1. Thailand—History—1945–
—Juvenile fiction [1. Thailand—History—1945- —Fiction] I. Title.
PZ7.H633Ri 1987   [Fic]   86-33745 ISBN 0-688-06355-1

To those who were killed
at Thammasart University
on October 6, 1976,
this book is respectfully dedicated.

Like rice without rain
We wilt in the parched fields,
Waiting to die a slow death
While others drain off our water.
Like the rice, like the wilting rice
We live waiting for the rain.
      (adapted from a Thai folksong)

RICE
WITHOUT
RAIN

FOREWORD

Minfong Ho's novel *Rice Without Rain* brings back many memories for me. Like the students in this novel, I first became aware of social problems within Thailand when I was a university student in Bangkok in the early 1970s.

As a little schoolgirl, I had thought that my country was a land of peace and plenty. *"Nai nam mi bla, nai na mi khao,"* we used to chant in our kindergarten class. "In the water there are fish, in the fields there is rice," we sang, and we believed it implicitly.

Later we were taught that Thailand was endowed with fertile farmland in the Central Plains and in the North, as well as with rich minerals and beautiful beaches all along the southern coastline. Over three quarters of the 50 million people of Thailand lived in these areas, most of them as rice farmers. We also learned that the Northeast was mountainous, drought-ridden, and poorer, but that region seemed as remote to me as the neighboring war-torn countries of Laos, Cambodia, and Vietnam.

The kingdom of Siam, as Thailand was traditionally known, was the only country in Southeast Asia never to have been colonized. During the centuries when the Spanish were the colonial masters in the Philippines, the Dutch in Indonesia, the British in Malaya and Burma, and the French in Indochina, only Thailand remained a free and independent country. In fact, the *Thai* in *Thailand* means "free."

Our transition from a feudal society based on an absolute monarchy to a more Westernized country was quite smooth (though of course not quite as rollicking as was made out in *The King and I!*). And Thailand went through the First and Second World Wars relatively unscathed.

By the time I was growing up in the 1950s and 1960s, major roads and railway lines had been built, airports and harbors expanded, high rises and factories mushroomed. Thailand seemed to be well on its way to modernization. Little did I realize then that this development benefited only a small section of the Thai population—the urban elite—leaving the lives of the farmers unchanged.

I held on childishly to my belief that everything was fine in Thailand, that there was plenty of rice and fish for everybody.

When I entered university, I started to question all this. If everything was fine, why were there slums sprawled right next to luxury hotels in Bangkok? Why were thousands of landless farmers streaming into the cities to look for jobs that didn't exist? Why did ragged women haul mud to build yet more roads while sleek ladies rode by in chauffeur-driven limousines? And why, if we were supposed to be a democracy with our own elected members of Parliament, were the military strongmen so powerful? Raising such questions were many young teachers newly returned from Europe and the United States, who taught us the political theory behind catchwords like *democracy* and *liberty.*

I listened avidly to these theories and came to believe that Thailand could progress only when the Thai people could elect a representative government and share more equally in the new wealth. For that to happen, I thought that people had to be made politically aware and organized. Thousands of other university students also shared these beliefs.

In October 1973, I was among the students who organized huge demonstrations in Bangkok to protest the increasingly corrupt military dictatorship that had ruled Thailand for decades. Reinforced by a ground swell of popular support, we managed to topple the existing government. The three military strong men fled the country, and in their place a civilian government was set up. Like the more recent collapse of the Marcos regime in the Philippines, this sudden change of government opened up a new era for Thailand.

The next three years were busy and exhilarating ones for us. Never before in Thailand had students held such a powerful role in shaping the national policy. We helped organize strikes and trade unions; we protested the high land rent that tenant farmers paid; we demanded parliamentary elections—in short, we tried to build a new Thailand.

During that time, Minfong was teaching at a university in Chieng-Mai, in northern Thailand. Like many other teachers then, she often joined groups of students to live and work in the rural areas around them. During their frequent stays in these villages, they learned firsthand of the hardships of the farmers, particularly the landless ones who had to pay half of each rice crop as rent.

Aware of the same problem, I was primarily concerned with organizing farmer leaders into a political group. There were many different student groups working in rural Thailand and many different ways used to alleviate rural poverty. Minfong and I first met then, and although our approaches were somewhat different, I think we both felt from the very first that we were working toward the same end.

A wave of idealistic young people like us spread throughout the villages and factories of Thailand to learn about social problems there and to push for reforms. Naively, we thought that we could do anything, if we only tried hard enough.

This optimism ended very abruptly.

On October 6, 1976, the military regained total control. With almost no warning, a student demonstration within Thammasart University was stormed by right-wing mobs and soldiers. In the brutal massacre that followed, at least forty-six students were killed, hundreds badly wounded, and hundreds more arrested. Never in the long history of our country had Thais been so brutal to other Thais. As thousands watched in horror, students were lynched or burned alive, stoned, beaten, dragged along the roads before being killed. After that, martial law was again imposed.

In much the same way that the Chinese student leaders in Beijing fled or went into hiding after the brutal attack on the demonstrators in Tiananmen Square in June 1989, so my friends and I fled Bangkok in 1976. Many students joined the outlawed Communist Party of Thailand in the jungles of northeastern Thailand. My husband and I were among them.

The four years that I spent in the "revolutionary bases" in the jungle were harsh ones. I was no longer a student but a Communist guerrilla. I lived in makeshift camps where food and medicine were scarce. My life became interwoven with the many peasants who had also joined the Communist forces.

Even living side by side with these farmers, I felt as if there was a wide gap of understanding between them and me. In those mountain base camps, these farmers carried out the orders of the Communist leadership as unquestioningly as farmers before them had paid the high rents to their landlord. Used to tilling their fields in stoic silence, they were also used to accepting absolute authority absolutely. I could not. I constantly questioned the validity of the Communist leadership, and partly because such questioning was not allowed, I became disappointed and finally disillusioned with the Communists.

When my husband and I finally decided to leave, many of the peasants we had grown to know well decided to leave too. Under a general amnesty granted to Communists, I returned to Bangkok, while those farmers returned to their fields.

And the gap between us has widened still more. I became a PhD student at Cornell University in New York, in a world inconceivably remote from those farmers whose lives I shared for years. I often found myself haunted by memories of their quiet faces. Who were they? What did they really want? What did they believe? Or feel?

I tried to find some answer in the maze of bookshelves at Cornell's libraries, but amid the endless words about political movements and peasant rebellions of Southeast Asia, I couldn't help feeling that the peasants themselves have remained, as always, silent.

Minfong was at Cornell then too, and we would often talk about the Thai student movement and how it had affected our lives and our perceptions. Minfong was asking the same questions about these farmers that I was. But she tried to find her answer in her own way. By creating Jinda, a vibrant village girl whose life is caught up in the actual events of the student movement of 1973–76, Minfong was trying to explore the inner lives of these villagers. Through Jinda, through her courage and fear, her joy and grief, I can catch glimpses of what was hidden behind the quiet faces of the peasants so familiar and yet so distant from me. *Rice Without Rain* not only brings back memories for me. It is also a bridge to those villagers.

Jiranan Prasertkul
Bangkok, Thailand

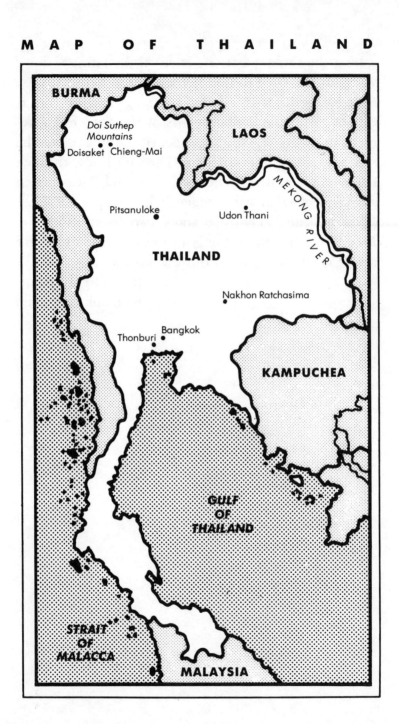

Heat the color of fire, sky as heavy as mud and, under both, the soil—hard, dry, unyielding.

It was a silent harvest. Across the valley, yellow rice fields stretched, stooped and dry. The sun glazed the afternoon with a heat so fierce that the distant mountains shimmered in it. The dust in the sky, the cracked earth, the shriveled leaves fluttering on brittle branches—everything was scorched.

Fanning out in a jagged line across the fields were the harvesters, their sickles flashing in the sun. Nobody spoke. Nobody laughed. Nobody sang. The only noise was wave after wave of sullen hisses as the rice stalks were slashed and flung to the ground.

A single lark flew by, casting a swift shadow on the stubbled fields. From under the brim of her hat, Jinda saw the bird wing its way west. It flew to a tamarind tree at the foot of the mountain, circled it three times, and flew away.

1

A good sign, Jinda thought. Maybe the harvest won't be so poor after all. She straightened, feeling prickles of pain shoot up her spine, and gazed at the brown fields before her. In all her seventeen years, Jinda had never seen a crop as bad as this one. The heads of grain were so light the rice stalks hardly bent under their weight. Jinda peeled open the husk of one grain: The rice grain inside was no thicker than a fingernail.

Sighing, she went back to work. A trickle of sweat ran down between her breasts and into the well of her navel. Her shirt stuck to her in clammy patches and the sickle handle was damp in her palm. She reached for a sheaf of rice stalks and slashed through it.

Reach and slash, reach and slash, it was a rhythm she thought she must have been born knowing, so deeply was it ingrained in her.

Out of the corner of her eye, she saw the hem of her sister's sarong, faded gray where once a bright flowered pattern had been. Dao was stooped even lower than the other harvesters and was panting slightly as she strained to keep up with Jinda.

From the edge of the field came the sudden sound of a thin, shrill wail.

"Your baby's crying, Dao," Jinda said.

Her sister ignored her.

"Oi's crying," Jinda repeated. "Can't you hear him?"

"I hear him."

"Maybe he's hungry."

"He's always hungry."

2

"Why don't you feed him, then?"

"Why don't you mind your own business?" Dao snapped.

"But couldn't you try?" Jinda insisted, as the wailing got louder. "I think you should at least try."

Dao slashed through a sheaf of stalks and flung them to the ground. "When I want your advice, sister," she said, "I will ask for it."

They did not speak again for the rest of the afternoon. The baby cried intermittently, but Jinda did her best to ignore him.

Jinda's thoughts drifted back to the harvest two years ago, before the drought. She and Dao had chatted away gaily then as they cut stalks heavy with grain. They had talked about what they might buy after the harvest—new sarongs, some ducklings, a bottle of honey. And as they talked, dark, handsome Ghan had sung love songs across the fields to Dao, until her face burned so red she had run down to the river and splashed cold water on it.

Ghan and Dao had been considered a perfect match by the whole village, since their fathers were the two most important men in Maekung. After all, wouldn't the marriage erase the long-standing hostility between Dao's father Inthorn, the village headman, and Ghan's father Mau Chom, the village healer?

So when Dao and Ghan were married, everyone in the village attended the wedding. All that morning each of the hundred or so families of Maekung had taken a

3

turn at tying the sacred thread around the bridal couple's wrists. Then, after the wedding feast of chicken curry and sticky rice, the dancing had begun. Countless couples, young and old, had danced the *ramwong* until the moon rose high above the palm trees.

There had been so much of everything then. So much food and rice wine, so much music and movement, and best of all, so much laughter.

Yet now, just two bad harvests later, there was never any laughter, nothing but the whisper of sickles against dry stalks in parched fields. Ghan had left to work in the city before his son was born, and Dao—poor Dao, Jinda thought, as she stole a glance at her sister's grim face—Dao had become just a shadow of herself.

When twilight finally came, the line of harvesters broke up and the men and women straggled back to the edge of the fields. Most rested against little thatched lean-tos, fanning themselves with their hats, while others ladled water from rusty buckets and drank deeply.

Jinda tucked her sickle into the waist of her sarong and approached her sister.

"Want to go down to the river?" she asked.

"Too tired," Dao said, massaging her back with one hand.

"You can stretch out under the banyan tree on the riverbank."

"And the baby?"

4

"Bring him. He likes the cool water, you like bathing him—and me, I like watching the two of you together."

Dao smiled then, and Jinda knew their quarrel was over. "All right," Dao said, "I'll go get the baby."

Jinda watched her sister duck into the lean-to where the baby was. As she waited for Dao to emerge, her father walked up to her.

"Tired?" Inthorn asked quietly.

"You are the one who should be tired, Father," Jinda said, smiling. "I saw you help others carry their loads of rice stalks."

"No more than usual. But I guess I'm not as strong as I used to be," Inthorn said, rubbing his shoulder ruefully.

Jinda longed to massage her father's shoulders for him but knew that she was too old to do that now. There had been a time years ago, shortly after her mother had died, when she massaged his shoulders every evening after he came back from the fields. He would sit on the top step of the porch, and she would kneel behind him, deftly easing away the tight knots from his shoulders, as he talked quietly of the day's work, much as he had with Jinda's mother before she died. After Dao had married and moved away to live in her father-in-law's house, Jinda had grown even closer to her father, taking over the chores of preparing meals and laying out the sleeping mats.

"Could we have dinner a little late tonight, Father?" Jinda asked now. "Dao and I are going down to bathe in the river."

Inthorn frowned. "Why don't you two forget about the river today?" he asked.

"Why? Are you very hungry?"

"I would rather you come straight home, that's all," he said.

"But why?"

Inthorn hesitated. "It is getting dark."

Jinda laughed in surprise. "But it's no darker than when we usually go."

"Still, you never know what strangers you might meet there."

"Strangers? But Father, I have never met a stranger there in my whole life! What are you talking about?"

For answer Inthorn pointed west, where the setting sun glowed behind the Doi Suthep mountain range. Silhouettes of gnarled teak trees stood, stark and motionless, against the sky.

"I don't see anything," Jinda said.

"On the nearest ridge," her father answered, pointing. "Halfway down the Outbound Path. Can't you see?"

The Outbound Path linked their small valley with the road through the mountain range, which merged with the big highway leading to the bustling town of Chieng-Mai nearly fifty miles away. Curious, Jinda scanned the winding path.

"There's nobody—" Jinda began, then broke off. She saw a small group of people, carrying what looked like heavy backpacks, climbing down the hillside.

"How strange," Jinda said softly.

These people were on foot. The few peddlers who came to their village always rode motorcycles, and the rent collector always roared in on his truck. Even the poorest farmer would have used a bullock cart or bicycle to travel the long path into their valley. "They're walking down," Jinda said. "Who could they be?"

Inthorn shook his head. "I don't know," he said, "but I don't like it."

Jinda understood. There had been frequent radio reports of Communist insurgents raiding villages in the area. She glanced up at the small figures on the hillside and frowned. Perhaps it wouldn't be a good idea to go bathing in the river, after all, Jinda thought.

Just then Dao stepped out of the thatched shelter. In her arms was her baby, wrapped snugly in a homespun cloth. "Here's Oi—all ready for a cool bath," Dao said. "Come, let's go!"

Jinda and her father exchanged a quick look. It was rare that Dao looked so eager anymore. "All right, go ahead," Inthorn said reluctantly. "But be sure to be home before dark."

As Dao walked on ahead, Jinda turned to look back at the Outbound Path. Even in the dimming light, the strangers kept up a brisk pace and were approaching the foot of the mountain. At their rate, Jinda thought nervously, these people would reach the river just before nightfall. She quickened her own step and hurried past her sister.

Feathery ashes from brush-fires on the mountainside had blown down, speckling the bamboo leaves fallen on the path below. At the end of the path was the river, a ribbon of cool silver under the bamboo groves.

Jinda reached the river first and stood on the bank waiting for Dao. It was shady there, screened off from the afternoon sun by a web of branches. A salamander slithered across a rock and into a patch of ferns.

Dao arrived and laid her baby down on the riverbank. Turning away from Jinda, she unbuttoned her shirt and peeled the sweaty cloth from her back. With a deft twist, she untied the knot of her sarong and pulled it up over her breasts. Wrapping the cloth tightly around her, she knotted the sarong.

Jinda shrugged off her own shirt and knotted her sarong around herself, aware that her own breasts were still smooth and firm and that her sister's had already started to sag.

She watched Dao cradle the baby as she waded into the river, tiny ripples fanning from her ankles. In midstream, where it was now only knee-deep because of the drought, Dao carefully sat down, hugging the baby to her. The clear water tinted her sarong a deep green.

"It's cold!" Dao laughed. For an instant she looked lovely and carefree again.

8

Jinda waded out and sat down next to her. The baby was lying half immersed in the cloth hollow of her sister's lap. Dao trickled handfuls of water over him. The baby cooed, shining sleek and slippery in the sunlight, and Dao crooned back to him. She pulled him gently to his feet, where he wobbled on thin legs for a second, then collapsed with a splash back into her lap.

"Poor Oi, poor little Oi," Dao said softly. "Why can't you stand straight?" She ran her hands over his frail legs. "Look at you, so skinny now," she murmured. "Newborn, you were soft as dough. And your hair— why has it turned so dry and brown, like straw?" She stroked the hair on his big head, careful not to tug at it. Recently tufts had come off in her hands.

Jinda watched in silence as Dao slid her hands down the baby's neck and over the stomach that bulged below his ribs. "And your belly," she said. "It's the only part of you that keeps growing while the rest of you keeps shrinking. Why, Oi, why?" Although her voice was still gentle, the gaiety was gone from it.

"It's not because you're hungry, little one, is it? I feed you spoon after spoonful of rice gruel, until you don't want a drop more. Is it milk you want, then? Is it?"

She loosened her sarong and turned slightly away from Jinda. Cradling the baby in her arms, she guided his mouth toward her right breast.

Jinda held her breath and tried not to look. Dao had

9

become shy about breast-feeding since her milk had begun to dry up. For the first four months Dao had suckled her baby openly, but as the baby's appetite increased, Dao grew thinner and her milk supply lessened. No matter how frequently she tried to feed him, he always fretted for more, kneading her breasts with tiny fists.

He was whimpering now, his face screwed into a pout as he sucked. It was no use. There was no milk. He started to howl.

With a deep sigh, Dao plucked the baby away from her nipple and rocked him soothingly against her. Gradually he calmed down, his cries subsiding into little hiccups.

"I'm sorry, baby," Dao told him. "Please understand. I can't help it. I just don't have enough milk." The baby gazed back at her with hollow, long-lashed eyes.

Just then, a single sunbeam filtered through from the mesh of branches above them and shone on Dao's face. The baby gazed at it, fascinated. He reached out a shaky arm to touch the patch of sunlight, patting his mother's dappled cheek.

Dao laughed with delight. "Jinda, look!" she called. "He's patting me, he's trying to comfort me."

"But he is only—" Jinda began in protest, then stopped.

She had seen a sudden movement behind the

branches of the banyan tree on the far side of the river. She had also heard something.

"What is it, Jinda?" Dao asked nervously.

A stranger stepped out of the shadows and stood, towering over them, on an overarching root of the banyan tree. For a long moment he looked at them in silence.

Then, slowly he raised both hands, palms together, and inclined his head in the traditional Thai greeting.

"Sawadi krup," he said. Although his voice was deep and solemn, there was a faint trace of a smile on his lips.

Jinda returned neither the greeting nor his smile. "What do you want? Who are you?" she asked sharply.

"I am sorry if I startled you. We mean no harm," he said quietly. "We—my friends and I—have been walking most of the day, and we're tired," he said. He glanced behind him, and Jinda could see three other figures in the shadows. "And since it's almost nightfall, we wondered if we might spend the night in your village. You . . . ," he studied Jinda with interest, "you are from the village nearby, aren't you?" He spoke with a distinct urban accent, which Jinda found disquieting.

The baby began to whimper, and Dao hugged him to her more tightly.

"You're not welcome here," Jinda said, her voice trembling slightly.

"But why?" The stranger smiled, and his teeth gleamed in the fading light.

The baby was crying now, and Dao looked scared.

"I think you . . . you had better leave, all of you," Jinda said.

"Isn't that a decision only the headman of the village should make?" the stranger asked, still smiling. He jumped down lightly from the banyan-tree root into the water and waded toward them. "Who are you," he asked Jinda mockingly, "to speak for the village headman?"

Jinda stood up and drew herself to her full height. Even so, she barely reached his shoulder. "I am Jinda Boonrueng," she said evenly. "His daughter."

For a second the stranger stared at her. Then he averted his eyes, but not quickly enough to hide a flash of interest.

Suddenly self-conscious, Jinda pulled her sarong higher and turned away. With as much dignity as she could manage, she helped Dao up, and together the two sisters waded back to their side of the riverbank. There they gathered their strewn clothes and hurried down the path toward the village.

Though Jinda never looked back once, she thought she could feel the stranger's gaze burn into her. No one had ever looked at her with such intense interest before. She found it disturbing, yet oddly exhilarating as well.

"What a strange young man," Dao murmured as they

walked along the path. "He sounded as if he's well educated, and from Bangkok. I wonder what he's doing here?"

"I don't know, and I don't care," Jinda said. "I just hope he doesn't stay." She was glad for the lengthening shadows that hid her face, so that her sister could not tell she was lying.

Jinda ran a quick hand down her thigh. The sarong was still slightly damp and felt cool against her skin. She had changed into a fresh white blouse and was now twisting her hair into a bun.

It's not as if tonight were the Loy Krathong festival, Jinda thought. Why am I bothering with my hair? Her reflection smiled knowingly at her from the little mirror on the veranda. Because you want to look pretty, it seemed to say.

Jinda had never been interested in looking pretty. She knew, studying herself in the mirror now, that her eyes were big, her eyelashes long, her complexion smooth and fair. A typical northern Thai beauty, Jinda told herself, and grinned. It was her grin that spoiled it. She had been told often enough to smile demurely. "Don't laugh with all your teeth showing!" Dao would say. But Jinda couldn't help it. Other village girls learned to smile sweetly because it made them pretty. Jinda laughed when she thought something was funny, which was far too often for her sister's taste.

Although Dao had often chided Jinda for her unfeminine ways, their father had never minded. In fact, he always treated her like the son he had yearned for before Pinit was finally born. He had taught her to fly a kite, to wield an ax, and to read from old newspapers. Even though, like the other village girls, Jinda had attended the district school for only four years, she could read and write better than many of the men in the village.

Other girls might spend leisurely afternoons threading jasmine buds through their hair, but Jinda would join the village elders as they discussed the latest headlines or listened to the news over the radio.

Of course Jinda admired the teasing grace with which her sister flirted with the village boys, but she never wanted to be like Dao. She admitted to herself that flirting looked like fun, with its soft laughter and quick whispers. But what did it lead to? A howling baby within a year and an unbroken cycle of swollen bellies and milk-heavy breasts after that. Jinda had seen that happen to her sister and countless other village girls, and she vowed that she would not let the same thing happen to her.

Yet now she found herself preening before the mirror. *I would even tuck a white gardenia in my hair if*

15

there were any in bloom, Jinda thought. She smiled, and was surprised how grown-up and pretty she looked with her hair deftly coiled at the nape of her neck.

Pausing to pick up the little oil lamp at the edge of the veranda, Jinda hurried down the stairs and toward the temple. She was late, and the temple was on the outskirts of the village, a good ten-minute walk away. Her father, grandmother, and little brother had all headed there as soon as they had heard about the four strangers gathered in the courtyard. Jinda, using her wet clothes as an excuse, had lagged behind to change and comb her hair.

A cool evening breeze blew against her bare arms. Jinda shivered, shielding the single flame of the lamp with her hand. It was early March, the end of the dry season, and the night air was pleasantly cool.

In the distance she could hear the sweet tinkling of the tiny bells hung high on the wooden temple eaves. A crescent moon was suspended above the mountains and a few fireflies darted among the orange blossoms of the flame-of-the-forest trees.

As Jinda approached the temple, she saw that a fire had been lit in the courtyard. The light of its flame flickered on the brick walls, casting into relief the sweeping temple roof arching above. Quite a few of the villagers must already have gathered here, Jinda thought, for there to be such a big bonfire.

She slipped past the temple gates into the courtyard.

There were about fifty people around the fire. Wrinkled old faces inset with eyes that glittered like bits of tile from the temple roof, glossy-faced boys with their shoulders wrapped in homespun shawls, young women hugging babies limp with sleep—everyone waited silently by the fire.

On the other side of the fire, sitting next to Inthorn, were the four strangers. As Jinda edged her way around the fire to her father, one of the strangers looked up and smiled at her.

Jinda caught her breath. It was the one who had spoken to her at the river. He looked even more striking now. Calm and at ease despite the stares of the crowd, he sat with his legs folded under him, like a tiger, watching her.

"Now that we are all here," he said, looking across the fire at Jinda, "I would like to begin the meeting."

For a second Jinda thought he was talking to her, but then she realized that he was addressing her father, who was seated between them. Relieved, she quietly sat down next to Inthorn.

"Please start," Inthorn said formally. "We would like to hear what you have to say."

"I had thought I would start by introducing each of us," the stranger said. His gaze seemed to seek Jinda out and focus on her. "But perhaps a better way to start is to sing a simple song that might tell you about us better than any formal introductions could."

He nodded briefly at the other three strangers and then, taking a deep breath, he began to sing.

His voice was slow and deep, almost a chant, and in the stillness it spiraled up to the trees canopying the fire. One by one, hesitantly at first and then with more vigor, the three other strangers joined in, until the chorus of their combined voices spilled out into the night air, replacing the whir of the cicadas.

Jinda hugged her knees and listened, entranced. She had never heard anything like this in her life. Yet the song seemed hauntingly familiar.

The song was the song of rice. It sang of the sowing of the unhusked seed rice and of the careful transplanting of seedlings from seedbeds to newly plowed fields. It sang of months of weeding, of watering, of waiting as the stalks grew tall and green, and then ripened into a dry brown. It sang of the days spent harvesting and threshing, winnowing and milling the grain—all to fill a single rice bowl.

> Each grain of rice is a bead of sweat.
> Each bead of sweat is a drop of pain.
> What fills the rice bowls of the rich?
> The sweat of our brow, the blood in our veins.

The song rippled outward, so that the night air seemed to pulse with its rhythm. Then the last note died away, low and solemn. Nobody moved. The circle of faces around the firelight glowed like embers fanned by a gust of wind.

Jinda, too, sat absolutely still. The song had struck

a deep chord in her, as if something long dormant had now stirred. There was pain in that song, a pain that had taken on new dignity because it had been given shape and acknowledged.

Nor was Jinda the only one to be so affected. She saw her father stare at the young stranger with a dazed expression. Then Inthorn reached over and took the stranger's hand. He held it up toward the firelight and studied the palm for a long moment.

"I don't understand," Inthorn said at last. "Your hand is smooth and soft, a student's hand. Yet your song," he shook his head in wonder, "your song is a farmer's song. It sings of our life. How could you know what it is like for us?"

"The song was written by a man called Jit Pumisak," the stranger replied. "Jit was from a noble family in Bangkok but chose to spend his life working among poor farmers in the Northeast. We have learned many of his songs, but we still don't know much of the life of the Thai farmers. That is why we are here. We hope to learn from you."

"Who are you?" Inthorn said cautiously.

"We are students from various universities in Bangkok," the stranger replied. "Jongrak and Pat," he gestured to the two young men on his left, "are from Chulalongkorn University. And Sri, beside me here, is a medical student from Mahidol." The person on his right looked up and smiled shyly. Jinda saw with surprise that, despite the short hair and jeans, she was

19

a girl, a frail, scholarly-looking girl. She had on thick glasses, which reflected the firelight, and her pale cheeks were tinted a slight pink by the fire. She looked up when he introduced her, squinting through her glasses as her blush deepened.

"As for myself," the stranger continued, "I am a third-year student at Thammasart University."

"And your name?" someone from the crowd prompted.

"Ned," he said.

"Just . . . Ned?" The question sounded sly, as if it were a trap. Jinda turned and saw Mau Chom, the village healer. Sitting beside him was her sister Dao, his daughter-in-law. Jinda wished Dao had sat next to their father instead.

"My full name is Nedmanoon Angkulprasert," the stranger answered easily, "but I doubt that anyone would have occasion to use it."

A group of girls giggled appreciatively, and Ned flashed them a quick smile.

Then he continued to explain that all four of them had come from the city and knew very little about village life. "We feel that as students, we should learn more of how the farmers of our country live." He paused and scanned the faces around the fire. "We are asking permission to live here in Maekung with you for the next few months."

There was a silence as the villagers waited for their headman to speak. Inthorn frowned. "What you are asking for is unusual," he said at last. "No one, certainly not university students from Bangkok, has ever wanted to just stay here before. What for? What do you want to do here?"

"We want to work alongside you when you work and learn about the problems you face. We want to understand what it is like to be a farmer in Thailand."

Inthorn looked more perplexed than ever. "But why? What do you *really* want?"

"I just told you, sir," Ned said with a trace of exasperation. "What more do you want to know?"

"He wants to know," Mau Chom broke in hoarsely, "whether you are Communists."

There. It was out. The word had crept into every villager's mind as soon as news had spread of the strangers' arrival in Maekung. *Communist*—the word sent a shiver down Jinda's spine. She had often heard radio reports of Communist guerrillas burning villages to the ground, killing children, and raping women. She stole a look across the fire at Ned. Could he be a Communist?

"Are we Communists?" Ned picked up a twig and poked the fire thoughtfully. "I think that question needs to be answered by more than just a simple *yes* or *no*," he said. "Instead, I would like to tell a story— of what has brought us here to Maekung. It is a rather long story." He glanced up at Inthorn questioningly. "May I tell it?"

Inthorn nodded. More wood was added to the fire.

21

Mothers shifted their dozing babies into a more comfortable position, and village youths sat up expectantly.

"You must all have heard of the student-led demonstrations of October 14 two years ago and the political changes that resulted," Ned began.

"Politics?" a girl echoed, sounding disappointed. "That's just games of the city. They have nothing to do with us." There were murmurs of assent.

"But they do, sister," Ned insisted politely. In a quiet voice charged with emotion, Ned described what had happened. During those demonstrations, he said, the people of Bangkok had come out to join the students by the hundreds of thousands, to protest the corruption of the military dictatorship that had been ruling Thailand for decades.

"Housewives, factory workers, shopkeepers, everyone came out to join us," Ned continued. "Bus drivers gave free rides to people who went to the Democracy Monument, where our demonstrations were held. Restaurant owners hauled pots of free food for us. Hospitals set up first-aid tents staffed by volunteer doctors and nurses. We had never expected such overwhelming support."

Neither had the government, Ned said. They clamped down on the demonstrators on the fourth day, sending out soldiers. There had been a mad stampede as the soldiers circled and then fired into the crowd. Martial law was imposed that night.

But that had not stopped the demonstrators. They had regrouped under cover of darkness and burned police boxes to the ground, cut telephone wires, and lobbed homemade bombs at patrolling police cars.

The fighting intensified, and the government called out the tanks. "At first, when we saw the line of tanks rumble down the avenue to the Democracy Monument, we did not believe they would shoot at unarmed people on the sidewalks," Ned said. "We were wrong."

The staccato fire of the tank guns mowed down countless pedestrians, and there was total confusion as the crowds dispersed. Some risked their lives carrying wounded strangers to safety, others linked hands and stood in front of soldiers begging them not to shoot their fellow citizens. The fighting escalated, and Bangkok was plunged into chaos.

That night, the three ruling army generals boarded a private plane and fled the country. A temporary civilian government was established, with a new constitution and free elections promised within the year.

"We had won," Ned said, his eyes glowing in the firelight. "It had been a hard struggle, and many lives had been lost, but we had won."

The villagers stared into the fire, as if searching for glimpses of the bloody street battles they had just heard about.

At last someone stirred. Jinda's grandmother reached for a burning twig and lit her home-rolled cigar with it. With deliberation she drew on the cigar, then puffed out some smoke. "That was a nice story," she said kindly. "But I don't understand. What did you win?"

One of the other students, Pat, spoke up. "Why, we won the right to a democratically elected government representative of the interests of the people," he said enthusiastically.

"And we won the chance to push forward reforms for workers and farmers, like a minimum-wage law and a lower land rent," Jongrak, the other student, added.

"And a better social service program, which would include better educational facilities and health care, especially in the rural areas," the medical student, Sri, said breathlessly, her voice soft but clear.

Someone laughed. It was a full, throaty laugh that Jinda immediately recognized as her grandmother's. Her face tanned and wrinkled like an orange peel left out in the sun to dry, the old woman peered across the fire at the students. "You all sound like old Buddhist monks chanting Pali scriptures," she said. Jinda heard sympathetic chuckles in the crowd. They had not understood a word either.

Ned straightened up then, drawing the attention back to himself with that one slight movement. "The story of October 14 has many meanings," he said quietly. "And what we have won, what Thailand has won, are many things. But the basic idea behind all of them is very simple." Ned leaned back and looked at Jinda's grandmother, as if he were speaking only to her. "It's as simple as plowing the fields after a bad harvest, or digging a new well when the old well has dried up. What we have won for our country, grandmother, is the chance to start over again."

It was quiet. Across the dying flames the old woman gazed at Ned. Age had pared away superfluous layers of flesh from her face and left the stark simplicity of skin over bone. As Jinda watched, her grandmother broke into a slow smile, the crinkles fanning out at the corners of her eyes.

"I like you," she told Ned. "You are so young." Her smile broadened, and with that one smile, the strangers were finally welcomed into Maekung.

T H R E E

The next morning, Jinda got up when the sky was barely light. She wanted to start the cooking fire and have a good breakfast ready for Sri, their house-guest.

The night before, Inthorn had finally given permission to the four strangers to stay on in Maekung. Once his decision was made, several families had graciously offered to take the students into their own homes. Inthorn had assigned three of the students to stay with a different family each. Then, courteously, he had invited Sri to stay in his own home, pointing out that he had a daughter about the same age as she was. Sri had been quick to accept and had flashed Jinda a shy smile across the fire.

Thinking of Sri's smile, Jinda gave the cooking pot a quick stir, and wished that she had some fish or pork to put in the stew. Still, the lemongrass and basil gave the strips of eggplant a nice fragrance.

Across the open veranda, in the main part of the house, the others were stirring. Jinda heard her grandmother putting away the sleeping mats and mosquito nets and caught a glimpse of her climbing down the veranda stairs. Jinda saw with surprise that Sri, looking slightly rumpled but as pale and delicate as the evening before, was right behind the old woman.

"Come, I will show you around," Jinda heard her grandmother say with a touch of pride. "You say you have never been in a village before?"

"Never," Sri answered.

"Poor child. Always stuck inside a classroom, aren't you?"

"Well, actually," Sri said hesitantly, "I spent last summer in Europe and the vacation before that in New York."

Jinda shook her head. She wasn't sure if Sri was bragging or apologizing.

Then Jinda heard her father descend to feed the buffalo tethered below the house. Last to get up was little Pinit, his light footsteps pattering across the wooden floorboards of their veranda.

27

Jinda called out to him. "Draw some more water from the well, Pinit! The urn up here is almost dry. And please fill the drinking jar too."

Pinit stuck his head in the kitchen. "Can't I do that later, sister?" he asked. "I want to watch that new girl with Granny."

Jinda always found it hard to refuse her five-year-old brother anything. "Well, all right," she conceded. "But don't get in their way." She resisted an urge to set aside her cooking and join them and see how Sri might react to the tour of the village.

Jinda was just soaking the rice and wishing that the grains weren't so broken, when Pinit burst through the door.

"Sister, come quick!" he panted. "It's Granny! Hurry!"

Jinda dropped her ladle and dashed out the kitchen door after him. "Is she hurt?" she asked. "Did she fall again?"

For answer Pinit pointed dramatically across the veranda toward the well.

Their grandmother was standing transfixed by the mango tree, her hands stretched out as if grasping at the air.

"I see a butterfly!" she shouted. "With yellow stripes. Oh, my, isn't it beautiful?"

Jinda rushed down the stairs and ran toward the old woman. Only when she was a few feet away did she notice that her grandmother had something in front of her eyes. It glinted in the morning sunlight.

"Granny, what are you doing?" Jinda asked. Sri turned to squint nearsightedly at her, and Jinda suddenly realized that her grandmother was wearing Sri's glasses.

"I can see!" the old woman said. With mounting excitement, she pointed out a flock of rice birds, a palm frond waving in the breeze, a group of children playing marbles in the sand. Her face, as creased as old leather, was wreathed in a huge smile.

"It's these eye-rings," she finally said to Jinda. "They are amazing! They sharpen the shapes of everything." She adjusted the slant of the glasses this way and that, peering through them all the while. "They are best this way," she decided, clamping the glasses on the tip of her nose and gazing about with her whole face tilted up. "There now. Sharp, very sharp."

Then she hobbled back to the hedge and picked a hibiscus blossom from it. Carefully, she peeled off each petal and stuck the remaining yellow pistil on her nose. Face upturned, the old woman laughed in delight, balancing both the drooping pistil and the glasses at the end of her nose.

Jinda laughed to see her grandmother clowning about like any village child. Impulsively, she ran over and grasped the old woman's hands in her own.

"Granny, let *me* give you a tour of the village! Let's

29

go!" Jinda said. Hand in hand, she and her grandmother walked out the gate and down the village path.
Sri stumbled behind, squinting in the morning sunlight.

Jinda's grandmother paused in front of Sakorn's
house. Adjusting the angle of the glasses, she studied
the sagging roof and broken fence. "Has that Sakron
grown so lazy," she said, "that he doesn't even repair
his house anymore?"

A few steps later she stopped again. "And why," she
asked, "is Sangad's storage barn crumbling? Isn't he
worried that the rats will get at the rice? And what
has happened to his wife's spice garden? Why is it all
dried up?"

Jinda tried to pull her away, but her grandmother
stood firm. She pulled her hand away from Jinda and
confronted Sri.

"What magic is in these eye-rings of yours?" the old
lady asked Sri. "If it is bad magic, why do I see the
hibiscus and the butterflies and clouds and mountains?" She shook her head, bewildered. "But if it is
good magic, why do I see my friends' homes so run-
down and neglected?"

"It is not magic, grandmother," Sri said gently.

"What is it, then?"

Sri hesitated. "Optics, I guess," she said.

The old woman grunted. "Some people call crows
ravens," she retorted.

Leaving the two girls behind, she walked back

through the swinging bamboo gate into their own yard. In a corner of the yard stood a little spirit house on a pedestal. The miniature wooden house had once been sturdy, with a gilt-edged roof and varnished walls. But the roof had caved in now, and its walls were bleached and warped. On the altar in front of it, a jar of joss-stick stubs stood next to some withered jasmine buds. These were the only offerings.

Leaning on her cane, the old woman peered up at the spirit house. "No rice, no candles, no fresh fruit?" she said. Her voice trembled. "Jinda, how can you neglect the guardian spirits of our home like this? What would your mother say? You promised her you would care for the spirit house after she died. Why haven't you, child? There aren't even any candles."

Jinda swallowed hard. "We can't afford to buy any," she said. "You know that, Granny."

"But some bananas, a few tangerines? A lime or two?"

"We saved what few fruits we had for Dao's baby," Jinda said. "There is a drought. You know that too."

"Surely a handful of rice . . . ?"

"Father says that if we do not have enough for ourselves," Jinda said shakily, "none can be spared for the spirits."

There was a long moment of silence. Then, wordlessly, the old woman took off the glasses and handed them back to Sri.

They walked to the house in silence. With her glasses

back on, Sri looked around with interest. When they reached the house, Sri examined it closely. Jinda became acutely aware that her home, like the spirit house, was in disrepair. The thatched roof sagged and its walls were bleached a bone gray by the sun. The thick pilings on which the house rested were worm-ridden and scarred by criss-crossing ruts where termites had chewed tunnels and laid their eggs. The wattle shed where the rice was kept had gaping holes gnawed by rats, holes that Inthorn hadn't bothered to repair because there was no longer any rice to store inside.

Even the pigpen under the rice barn, once so full of squealing, squirming piglets, was deserted.

"So this is your home," Sri said quietly.

Home? The word sounded strained to Jinda. For the first time in her life, she felt ashamed of where she lived.

The smell of the lemongrass stew simmering in the kitchen reminded Jinda that breakfast was almost ready. "Come up for some food," she said, and started up the stairs to the veranda.

The floorboards upstairs were spotlessly clean, and the water jar was full. It wasn't their fault that the chicken coop was empty and the pigpen deserted. They had been forced to sell most of their animals because of the drought. They had done their best and really had nothing to be ashamed of.

And yet, Jinda resented the careful way Sri walked across the porch, as if afraid the planks might give way under her. When Jinda offered her a drink of water from the earthenware jar, Sri asked if the water had been boiled first, then politely refused when she heard it came straight from their well.

"I will help you boil some drinking water later," Sri said.

Go boil yourself, Jinda felt like saying. Instead, she stalked into the kitchen and furiously poked the cooking fire.

Sri followed her into the kitchen and stood for a while by the open window. Outside, a few ducks were waddling to the river, their sleek feathers brushed glossy shades of brown by the morning light. The small straw fire lit to keep the mosquitoes at bay sent a tendril of smoke spiraling up from under the hayloft. The buffalo was tethered nearby, placidly swishing its tail.

"How peaceful it is here," Sri said, smiling.

Jinda did not smile back. Squatting by the fire, she stirred the soup. The gleam of the embers cast flickering shadows on the walls.

Jinda wondered if she should add another handful of rice to the pot. She knew their storage bin was nearly empty, however, and with Sri now staying with them, their rice would have to be rationed out even more carefully. Still, this was their first meal together, and she did want there to be enough.

33

Before Jinda could decide what to do, Sri knelt beside her, her knees tucked primly together.

"I brought some rice with me," the student said. "And some salted fish. Shall I get them now?"

"No, you keep it," Jinda said, without looking up.

"But it is meant for you. Ned said we would be parasites if we didn't contribute our share of the food."

Jinda wondered what parasites were but didn't want to ask. "We have no need of it," she answered gruffly.

"Let me get it anyway." Sri stumbled awkwardly to her feet and rummaged in her backpack.

Jinda heard paper being rustled. She stared into the fire, determined not to look behind her.

"Where should I put the rice?" Sri asked.

"Anywhere you want."

Sri circled the room and paused by the shelves of jars of rock salt and dried chili. Jinda wondered if Sri would have the sense to pour the rice into the rice bin. Then Jinda heard the wooden cover of the bin sliding off. Sri had found it after all.

"It's empty!" Sri called out, her voice reverberating in the hollowness of the bin.

Jinda flushed. "No, it's not. There's still some left, at the very bottom," she said. "Anyway, we will have a lot more after the harvest."

"Yes?" Sri sounded uncertain.

There was a pause, then Jinda heard the sound of

rice being poured into the empty bin, a swift, constant drumming like the pattering of rain on a tin roof. Jinda yearned to look but forced herself to remain by the fire as the stream of rice continued. How much rice did that girl bring, anyway?

At last Jinda could resist no longer. She jumped up and watched the flow of the long, unbroken, plump grains. Her jaw dropped. It had been years since she had seen such beautiful rice!

Sri emptied the bag and, before Jinda could protest, crumpled it up and tossed it into the fire. Jinda watched the bag burst into flames, a thick brown sack without a single hole, wasted!

Attracted by the burning paper, Sri knelt by the fire. Then she peered into the pot. Beneath the pock-marked surface were some wilted leaves and lemongrass stalks. "What . . . what is it?" she asked, crinkling her nose in distaste.

Jinda stirred the lemongrass soup so fiercely that a few drops splattered out onto Sri's bare arm. "What do you think it is?" she snapped.

Taking out a starched white handkerchief, Sri wiped her arm. "It is food . . . isn't it?" she said uncertainly.

At that moment, Jinda hated the peanuts and tamarind leaves Pinit had gathered from the forest to add to the soup. She wished bitterly that she had some chicken instead, so she could have made a delicious curry to impress this Bangkok student with. "Of course it's food," Jinda said loudly.

Sri was still frowning. "Food . . . for us?" she asked.

Burning with shame, Jinda pulled the pot off the fire and shoved it into a corner. "No, it's food for the pigs!" she cried. "Didn't you see the big pigpen full of piglets in our yard?"

Sri's smile was one of sheer relief. "Yes, of course," she said.

Jinda stoked the fire without saying another word. Finally she filled another pot with water, scooped out five handfuls of the rice that Sri had brought, and poured them into the pot.

"Can I help?" Sri asked.

Can a rooster walk any faster with three legs? Jinda retorted silently. "We might as well have your salted fish too," she said, not looking at Sri. "You can cut me a piece of it."

Sri picked up another paper bag and pulled out a dried fish. Holding it with her thumb and forefinger, she turned it over gingerly. "I . . . how . . . where do I cut it?" she asked.

Jinda stared at her in disbelief.

"I mean . . . along the front, or back? Or down the middle?" The girl's voice faltered.

Without a word, Jinda took the fish from her and deftly sliced into it.

Sri watched helplessly. "Ned says Thai students don't use their hands enough," she mumbled. "He says that is one of the biggest problems of Thai intellectuals today. All we have ever been taught to do is think." Sri sounded as if she were reciting from a textbook.

Sure, Jinda said to herself. Then how come you never thought to look at our pigsty and see that it's empty?

The four students settled quietly into life in Mae-kung, and gradually their presence was accepted by the villagers. Each morning the students would set out with their hosts to join the harvesting in the fields. They had to be taught how to hold sickles and how to grasp rice stalks in one hand and slash through them with the other. They learned quickly and seemed not to mind the hard work.

Despite her initial misgivings, Jinda grew to like Sri. True, Sri worked very slowly, sawing clumsily with the sickle blade when a deft slash would have done. But even when her small, soft hands became badly blistered, she never complained. Jinda often claimed the place next to Sri in the row of harvesters, cutting a wider swath to help Sri with her work.

The April days grew hot and dry. Harvesting the dry-season rice crop had always been hot, dusty work, but it seemed especially grueling this year because of the drought. Strong morning breezes blew up swirling eddies of dust in the stubbled fields.

The day Lung Tong's field was being harvested, the wind was especially strong. The men were collecting sheaves of rice and tying them in huge bundles before hoisting them onto shoulder poles.

Jinda watched as she slashed through her swath of rice stalks. She had always liked the way the men moved, balancing the stalks on their shoulder poles as they loped across the fields to the threshing ground. But today she watched even more keenly because, for the first time, Ned was among them.

From under the brim of her straw hat, Jinda watched him. Even with the weight of rice stalks on his shoulder, he moved gracefully, having learned to walk with the long, rhythmic strides necessary to balance such a load. It looked effortless, but as he approached Jinda she saw that his forehead was beaded with sweat and his shirt soaked through. It didn't seem right to her that a university student with hands so smooth and uncalloused should do such work.

She watched Ned as he passed and smiled at him encouragingly. He looked at her, lost his footing, and stumbled.

"Careful!" Jinda cried, springing forward to steady him. For a second, their hands touched. Then he straightened up and hurried on. Jinda stood looking after him, aware of the sudden whispering around her.

Minutes later, two village youths carrying another

heavy sheaf of rice stalks between them walked by, one of them a short sturdy boy who had often tried to attract Jinda's attention. As they approached her, this boy pretended to totter backward, flailing his arms. "Careful!" the other boy called out, in shrill mimicry of Jinda, and steadied him lovingly. The girls harvesting nearby burst into loud giggles.

Jinda felt as if hot coals were being poured down her neck. For the rest of the day she was careful not to look at Ned again, much less speak to him.

Much less controversial was Jinda's growing friendship with Sri. Since the two girls were about the same age and sharing the same house, they took to spending much of their leisure time together.

In the cool of twilight after work, Jinda wandered down the quiet village paths with Sri, asking her questions about city life and introducing her to neighboring families. Shy and stuttering though Sri was with adults, she seemed quite at ease with children and laughed and played with them happily.

One evening when they were out strolling, Sri noticed that Nai Tong's youngest son had bloodshot eyes. His eyelids were puffy, and he kept rubbing them.

"What's the matter?" Sri asked him. "Have you been crying?"

The boy shook his head vigorously. "I never cry," he said.

"Are your eyes itchy then? They are? May I have a look at them?" Sri asked.

40

Obediently, the boy let Sri examine his eyes.

"Conjunctivitis," Sri told Jinda. Then she turned back to the boy and said, "Run home and ask your mother if I can put some drops into your eyes. It'll make the itch go away."

Soon the boy was back, his wary mother in tow. "What do you want to do with Bui's eyes?" she demanded.

Shyly, Sri mumbled a long explanation about infection and possible damage to the delicate retinas. The mother listened grimly.

"How much?" little Bui's mother asked.

Sri blinked. "Oh, it . . . it's free," she stuttered.

"Well, go ahead then," Bui's mother said.

A crowd of curious children had gathered by the time Sri came back with a vial of clear liquid. Jinda held the boy's head as Sri squeezed two drops into his eyes. "Come back tomorrow," Sri told him. "I will have to do this for a few days."

The next day, Bui brought along two other children with red eyes. "Their mothers said you can treat them too," he explained, "if it's still free."

Soon it was not just conjunctivitis, but skin rashes, stomach ailments, and chest colds. Each evening, when Sri and Jinda returned home from the fields, a growing collection of children, some with their mothers or older sisters, would be waiting for Sri underneath the veranda. Sri always treated each child carefully and never charged any money.

"Do you treat grown-ups, too?" Nai Wan's wife asked one night.

Sri hesitated for only a fraction of a second. "I will treat anybody who is sick," she said.

And so the next evening, at Inthorn's friendly suggestion, Sri set up a table in the temple courtyard, with a single kerosene lamp on it.

"A clinic," Sri breathed, and her eyes shone as she unpacked her bottles of medicine from a cardboard box. "I am actually starting a clinic. Oh, Jinda! I've dreamed of doing this for so long!"

Jinda smiled and helped Sri arrange her medicines in a neat row on the wooden table. "You're all set now," she told Sri. "I'll wait for you at home."

"Wait, don't go," Sri said. Nervously she looked at the groups of villagers already starting to gather around her table. "There are so many of them, and I . . . I don't understand their dialect sometimes. Please stay and help me."

Jinda hesitated. It was one thing for a university student from Bangkok to assume the role of doctor, but quite another for a young village girl to be healing people, especially since Mau Chom, the traditional healer in the village, had already expressed his hostility toward Sri. What would he think of Jinda's joining in? The fact that Mau Chom was Dao's father-in-law only complicated matters.

"I . . . I think I had better go home," Jinda said.

Sri's hand gripped her arm. "Jinda, please," she pleaded. "I'm nervous."

Jinda took a look at her friend and realized how much she liked her. "Of course, if you really want me to," she said, smiling.

The first person in line was Lung Teep, a wiry old man with ears that stuck out on either side of his head like little tree mushrooms. Lifting the cuff of his baggy trousers, he showed Sri a large, festering sore on his calf. Jinda held the lamp close as Sri opened the sore, drained off the pus, and applied some ointment. "Swallow one of these pills before you sleep every night," Sri said, handing him a little packet.

The old man took the pills with both hands. "Thank you," he said, then added, "Doctor."

Sri and Jinda exchanged a quick smile.

Many of the villagers who came had skin rashes, rough patches on their wrists and ankles where the fuzzy rice stalks had rubbed against bare skin. Some had wracking coughs and high fevers. And countless others had intestinal problems. Quietly and efficiently, Sri applied ointment, gave injections, and prescribed pills.

But there were also those who could not be cured by Sri's medicine. A lame young man, an old woman whose teeth were loose and rotten from chewing betel nut, a girl with a harelip, were among those who came to Sri's clinic during the next few weeks. Each was told there was no help available and gently turned away.

Jinda felt particularly bad about turning away Chart. He came late one evening, shuffling out of the shadows, his arms swinging loosely. Chart was one of the few village children who had studied at high school. Jinda still treasured a worn old geography textbook he had given her, with pictures of children in foreign countries in it. The year before, while he was back in Maekung during a school holiday, he had been struck down with a fever so high that no one thought he would live. He had survived but afterward could not talk coherently, or read and write. Instead, he wandered through the village, playing with the smallest children until even they chased him off.

As Jinda explained all this to Sri, she saw the medical student frown. "What does he want me to do?" Sri asked.

Chart made a series of guttural sounds.

"He wants to go back to school," Jinda interpreted for him. The boy nodded eagerly.

"So you had a high fever?" Sri asked. "And you turned hot and cold every few hours?"

Chart nodded again and again, his thick fingers gripping the table.

One by one Sri very gently pried his fingers up. "I can't help you, brother," she said. "You probably had malaria and have suffered brain damage caused by the fever."

The boy looked at her, his eyes round and trusting.

"There is nothing I can do for you. Nothing, understand?" She had worked his fingers off the table and now held his hand in hers. "Nothing," Sri repeated, blinking behind her thick glasses.

For a moment Chart stared at her. Then he turned to Jinda, who shook her head sadly. Finally, eyes downcast, he stumbled off into the shadows.

Sri's hands were clenched into tight little fists. "It is not my fault," she said, her voice strained. "How can I help people like him?" She pointed at the medicine in the cardboard box. "See that? It doesn't look like much, does it? I was in a group of medical students who made the rounds of every pharmacy in Bangkok, begging free medicine from the owners. Night after night we did this, until we had collected boxes of medicine. We filled the storeroom at the Student Union office with what looked like an enormous supply, enough to heal every sick child in the country, we thought. But when we divided up the medicine among the student groups going out to the villages, it didn't seem like so much anymore. Now," she pushed the battered box away wearily, "now it seems like nothing."

Quietly Jinda put her arm around Sri's bony shoulder. "Let's go home," Jinda said. "You are tired."

Sri's eyes had dark rings under them, obvious even behind the sheen of her glasses. But Sri shook her head and smiled. "Tired? When there're still people wait-

45

ing to see me? No, of course I'm not tired." Straightening her shoulders, she put her glasses back on and beckoned for the next patient to approach.

Sri continued to administer her clinic, and each day more people came. The lines grew longer, and since whole families would accompany the patient, a large group of people were gathered with nothing to do but wait. Ned saw his chance and built a small bonfire in the corner of the temple courtyard. There he invited the villagers to sit and talk, and before long he was leading a lively discussion far into the night.

As word got around the village that some very interesting ideas were being discussed around that fire, more and more villagers gathered there. Before long, Ned's fireside discussions were as much an established part of the village night life as Sri's clinic.

As Jinda helped Sri apply ointments and bandages, she listened closely to Ned and the farmers. The talk often revolved around the land rent. The harvesting was almost over and the threshing already begun. Sometime within the next few weeks, the rent collector would come in his truck and, in one afternoon, take away half of what they had spent five months to grow. Especially after a poor harvest like this year's, the farmers could ill afford to give up so much of their rice, and they worried about it.

Ned had no solution as neat as Sri's bandages, but he talked earnestly of countries where the land rent was only one tenth the value of the crop, and of other villages in Thailand where farmers were beginning to refuse to pay half of the crop as rent to the landlords. Inthorn often listened to these discussions but seldom joined in, preferring to keep his thoughts to himself.

One night, after the last of the patients had left, Jinda and Sri lingered by the kerosene lamp. A gust of night wind blew across the courtyard, tinkling the tiny bronze bells on the temple eaves. Only a handful of farmers remained around the dying campfire with Ned. A few phrases about the poor harvest and high rent drifted over to Jinda. Gradually, though, as the crowd of patients dwindled, the voices around the fire subsided. In the stillness of the night, the whir of cicadas grew louder.

Suddenly a lone woman emerged from the shadows of a big rain tree and walked toward Jinda. Head draped in a homespun shawl, her face was in shadow. Only after she entered the circle of lamplight around Sri's table did Jinda realize who it was.

"Dao!" she exclaimed in joy. "You've brought Oi!"

Dao stopped a few feet short of the table, hesitating. Their grandmother followed close behind, prodding her gently. Jinda realized that the old woman was the one who had convinced Dao to come.

"Yes? Can I help you?" Sri asked her.

The old woman stepped up, her smooth, thin shoulders gleaming in the lamplight. She took her cigar from

47

her mouth and tucked it behind her ear. "It is little Oi," she said, nodding toward the bundle in Dao's arms. "He is very sick."

When Dao made no move to hand over the baby, the old woman lifted him from her granddaughter's arms and held him out to Sri.

With both hands, Sri carefully took the bundle. She unwrapped the threadbare cloth and looked at the large, unblinking eyes staring up at her.

"His head is burning and he isn't hungry anymore," Grandmother said.

Dao spoke up then, her voice as soft as the night wind. "He doesn't want rice gruel, and he won't try to breast-feed now," she said softly. "And he never smiles when I sing to him anymore."

Sri's hands moved over the baby, probing, stroking, examining. She stopped and frowned at a large sore on his right arm. "What's this?" she asked.

"Just a mosquito bite," Dao said defensively. "Everyone has them. He has had several before, but this one doesn't heal."

Sri said nothing. Her face was grim. Telling Jinda to hold the lamp up, she peered into the baby's ears, pressing at his temples.

"His left ear is infected," she said as Oi whimpered. "That's probably the cause of his fever." Her hands strayed over the baby's bloated stomach, up his ribs, and to his thin stem of a neck. "Kwashiorkor," she said. "Marasmic kwashiorkor. So malnourished he doesn't have the strength to fight a simple infection." She looked up at Dao. "What do you feed him?" she asked.

Dao chewed at her underlip. "I . . . I do my best," she faltered. "Rice porridge mostly, and some mashed bananas when we have any . . ."

"Any milk?"

Dao turned her face away. "My milk ran dry weeks ago," she murmured, her voice low with shame.

"But your baby needs protein, and—"

"Oh, give him some then, please!" Dao eyed the bottles of medicine lined up neatly on the table.

"But I can't, it is . . ."

"Please, just a little?"

"You don't understand," Sri said, biting her lips. "Protein is not medicine. It is meat, fish, milk . . ."

"Meat?" Dao echoed, bewildered. "And fish?"

The two young women stared at each other for a long moment. Finally Jinda's grandmother spoke.

"We have no meat, no fish, no milk," she said abruptly. She relit her cigar with a twig dipped into the lamp and took a long puff from it. "When the paddies are knee-deep in rainwater, we can catch snails or soft-shelled crabs, and even some catfish." She blew out a stream of smoke and continued dreamily. "Or in the winter, we can go into the forest and find pink and white mushrooms under moist ferns, or cut the

49

spikes of newly sprouted bamboo shoots from the groves." She tapped the ash off her cigar. "But what is there now when the fields are cracked and hard and the mountainsides barren? Don't talk to us of meat and fish, child. We are hungry, all of us, but the little ones most of all."

Sri took off her glasses and rubbed her eyes wearily. "Of course," she whispered. "I should have realized."

The grandmother smiled. "Those eye-rings of yours, they are probably very good for reading books, but are they as good for seeing what's right in front of you?" She leaned forward and stroked the baby's cheek with a rough, wrinkled fingertip. "This is my first great-grandchild," she said quietly. "Can you help him?"

Sri looked very tired. "Medicine can cure the fever he has," she said, "but it won't help him grow to be a healthy boy." Sri held the baby out to his mother, but Dao stood with her hands by her sides, stubbornly refusing to take him back.

"Please," Dao said, "give him some medicine. Just a handful. He doesn't need much."

"I can give him a dose of antibiotics and some vitamins," Sri said quietly, "but that is not food."

Dao nodded and took Oi back, carefully wrapping him in the shawl again. With a bowed head she accepted a package of pills from Sri. Then she and her grandmother slipped back into the shadows.

Jinda lowered the wick of the kerosene lamp so that only a little circle of light surrounded them. Sri put her glasses back on and started to pack up the medicine.

"Neomycin, streptomycin, erythromycin," she chanted softly, reading off the label of each bottle as she capped it. "Tetracycline, penicillin, ampicillin . . . all this medicine," she said, putting the last bottle in the box. "All this medicine, and what use is it?"

The night was very still. The stars and fireflies had struck up their mute dialogue. Somewhere a lone dog howled in the night.

"Can doctors heal hunger, Jinda?" she asked quietly. "Will any amount of penicillin cure poverty?"

Jinda shook her head. She had not understood much of what Sri was saying, but in her heart she knew this much: little Oi was not going to get well. She felt lost and angry, but when she saw the bewilderment in her friend's eyes, she wanted to comfort her.

"You have helped many villagers already," Jinda said quietly.

"It is not the few villagers here and there who are sick," Sri said, as if talking to herself. "It is the whole society. Our country is sick—the whole country, and I'm just patching up a few people. What good is that? What use am I?"

Jinda blew out the kerosene lamp. In the darkness, she could see a few fireflies blinking among the tree leaves. For a while neither of them spoke. Then Jinda reached out and touched Sri's hand. "Nobody can be a lamp," she said slowly. "The most we can hope to

51

be is a firefly. And you," she squeezed the student's hand, "you have been a bright firefly."

They stood there a moment longer, watching the fireflies weaving pinpoints of patterns among the shadows. Then they picked up the kerosene lamp and box of medical supplies and headed home.

F I V E

Three days later, Dao's baby died.

There was no funeral, no monks came to pray, no special meal was cooked for the few mourners. His little body was simply placed in a rough coffin, where he looked even more fragile and shrunken than before.

He was cremated near the temple grounds in a clearing at the center of a grove of large bodhi trees. His ashes, like those of countless others before him, were scattered by the wind to the rice fields beyond.

Even after the cremation fire had died down and the embers were burning low, Dao remained seated against the trunk of a gnarled bodhi tree in the shady grove. Sri and Jinda and her grandmother, together with a few of the village women, sat nearby to keep her company.

A dragonfly glided down and alighted on Dao's arm.

Sri reached over to brush it away. "I am sorry about little Oi," she murmured, her hand on Dao's arm.

Dao flung Sri's hand off. "I am sorry, too," she snapped, "sorry that I didn't take my father-in-law's advice to stay away from you. You killed my child."

Jinda stared at Dao, amazed that the hard, shrill voice was that of her sister. Dao had sounded so angry and spiteful.

"I did all I could to help him," Sri stammered. "Surely you know that?"

"You didn't help him. You killed him!" Dao said in the same tight voice.

"But he . . . he was already dying, Dao," Sri said shakily. "I told you that. I said he was malnourished. Infants need milk—"

Dao seized on the last word. "Milk? You know my milk ran dry weeks ago. Are you blaming me?"

"Of course not," Sri said. "You're malnourished yourself. If you could have afforded better food. . . ."

But Dao was not listening. She got up, holding onto the bodhi tree for support. There was a dazed look on her face. "No, it is true. I am to blame," she said. "I had no milk."

"Dao, you are tired," Jinda said gently. "Come, let's go home now."

Dao did not seem to hear her. "Little Oi needed my milk, but I failed him," she insisted. She twisted the baby's old checkered shawl into a tight coil. "If I had

54

milk, he wouldn't have died. I am to blame, I am."
Her voice broke. With a choked sob, she ran out of
the bodhi grove. Her bare feet kicked up tiny swirls of
dust as she stumbled along the path up the hillside.

Jinda watched her, not knowing what to do. Then
she felt a nudge.

"Go after her, child," her grandmother said quietly.
"Your sister is without mother, without husband, and
now without child. You are the one closest to her now.
Go talk to her, Jinda," she said.

Jinda got up and walked out of the bodhi grove. The
sun was fierce and the sand hot between her toes as
she followed Dao's footsteps.

She found Dao sitting on a log under a tree, the
checkered shawl on her lap. Dao looked up but said
nothing as Jinda sat down beside her.

Tongue-tied, Jinda gazed at the scene below them.
In the dull glare of the afternoon sun, everything looked
dead. Only the stubble of the harvest was left, its few
stray stalks long since gleaned bare by scavenging
crows. The village was one flat, relentless shade of
brown. Brown dust on brown roads. Brown thatched
roofs over bleached cracked walls. Brown hay stacked
on dusty brown lofts. Brown leaves drooping from
gnarled brown trees. Everything was brown, brown.
Jinda felt that if death had a color, it would be brown.

"Dao," Jinda said awkwardly, "I am sorry that Oi
died."

Her sister remained silent.

"Please don't be sad," Jinda said. "You can have another baby."

Dao did not move. "Be quiet," she said coldly.

"But it's not so hard, is it? To have another baby?" Jinda plowed on. "You said before you liked being pregnant . . ."

"Quiet!" Dao ordered.

But Jinda did not know how to stop. "But you said you liked feeling him kick inside you, remember? You let me feel him. What a strong kick he had! Did it hurt, Dao? What did it feel like?"

"It felt all right," Dao said grudgingly, after a long pause. "It felt as if he was trying to touch me."

"And when he was born, did that hurt? They wouldn't let me see, you know."

"It hurt," Dao said. "He was a big baby. With fat hands and little soft ears just like his father's."

Dao talked then, her words slow and thoughtful, as if each one were precious. As she talked, she stroked the checkered shawl on her lap. "I bathed him in a bucket by the well at first. Do you remember?" Memory upon memory she dredged up and laid before Jinda: how she had suckled him, how he had first smiled at her, how he had held onto her thumb with both hands. Her voice gradually became lighter, and once she even smiled.

Jinda urged her on, wanting her to smile again. "And that time we took him bathing in the river," Jinda prompted, "the day the students came. Oi reached up and stroked your cheek, like this . . ." She leaned over and hesitantly placed her hand on Dao's face.

Dao held onto her sister's wrist and pressed her cheek onto Jinda's palm. Her tears came then, cool and swift and silent, trickling through Jinda's fingers and onto the shawl.

For a long while the sisters sat on the log, watching the afternoon shadows lengthen in the valley below them. Neither spoke much. Toward twilight they heard the familiar jingle of cowbells, faint and musical in the distance. They knew it was their little brother bringing the buffalo home, and so they got up and went down the hill to meet him.

In a subtle but pervasive way, Oi's death affected the entire village. Around their weaving looms, women sighed over how thin their own children were becoming. By the temple bonfire at night, men brooded over how little rice they would have left after paying the rent. And in all their conversations lurked the unspoken question: Whose child would die next?

Seeing the mounds of rice grain building up on the threshing ground day by day, Jinda knew that Dusit, the rent collector, would be coming soon. Filled with a growing sense of dread, Jinda wanted to talk to Ned about it. But Ned was always busy with the harvesting in the daytime and talking with the men around the fire in the evenings.

Jinda's chance came one quiet afternoon, however, when she was sitting by the riverbank. She had just bathed and was watching her little brother splash water on his buffalo. A magpie perched on the buffalo's back, pecking at insects as the huge animal swished its tail back and forth in a graceful arc.

A dry twig snapped behind her. She glanced around and saw Ned walking down the trail, a cloth towel draped around his shoulders.

"I see I will have to share my bath water with your buffalo," he said, smiling at Jinda.

Jinda tried to hide her pleasure at seeing him. "You could use the water upstream of him," she said lightly, not sure whether she should leave, now that he had announced his intention to bathe.

"I will just help your brother wash the buffalo for a start. How about it, Pinit?" Ned called out.

The little boy grinned. "Fine!" he said. "Come on in."

Jinda watched as Ned and Pinit scooped handfuls of water over the buffalo's legs, rubbing off patches of dried mud. The animal stood quietly between them, his eyes dreamy and unfocused.

"Nice placid animal you have there," Ned said conversationally, splashing some water onto the buffalo.

"You haven't seen him when he's riled up," Pinit retorted. "He can be a real fighter. Why, just today I was racing Cousin Daeng home from the fields when

Daeng steered his buffalo right in front of us, trying to block us off. My buffalo got so mad he charged straight ahead instead of slowing down, and we went through Lung Tong's fence!" He slapped the animal's flanks with pride. "It took four men dragging at the reins to slow him down."

Jinda shook her head. "Wait till Father hears about that," she said. "He'll want to drill his nose and insert a nose rein. Father has been complaining that the animal is getting out of hand."

Her brother shot her a worried look. "Do you really think so, Jinda? I won't race him anymore, I promise. I'll make sure he'll be obedient and tame."

"The only way to make sure of that is to drill his nose and lead him around with a rope through the nose," Jinda said grimly.

"No!" Pinit wailed. "I can train him. I can tame him."

"Tell that to Father," Jinda said. "He'll be after you when he hears about Lung Tong's fence."

"It is no use talking to Father," Pinit said morosely. "He's so moody these days he never listens to me anymore."

"Why?" Ned asked, suddenly alert.

Pinit shrugged. "Father is always in a bad mood before Dusit comes."

"Dusit? The rent collector?" Ned asked.

Jinda nodded. "Actually, Father is moodier than I

have ever seen him. The harvest has been so poor that after we give half of it to Dusit, we won't have enough for ourselves."

"Why do you have to give him half?" Ned said, scrubbing the buffalo.

Jinda stared at him in disbelief—the question seemed so silly she could hardly believe Ned had asked it. Yet when she tried to answer it, she had trouble finding the right words. "Why? Well, because . . . because that's just the way it is. We rent the farmland for half of the harvest, that's all."

"But why half?" Ned persisted, turning to face Jinda. "Why not less than half? Why not pay him a third of the harvest?"

"It . . . can't be done," Jinda said.

"Why not?" Ned countered.

Irritated, Jinda replied, "Because it's against the law."

"Is it?" Ned challenged. He waded over to where Jinda was and sat down next to her. "Is there really a law that states that the land rent has to be half of the crop?"

"There must be. That's how it has always been."

"Ah, but that is not the law. It is only tradition," Ned said.

"What's the difference? What matters is that we would be forced off the land." Keenly aware of how close Ned was sitting, Jinda dared not turn to look at him but spoke staring straight ahead. "We would just

60

be replaced by other tenant farmers who would pay the usual rent."

"Not if all of Maekung acts together, with each farmer paying only one third as rent," Ned argued. "The landlord can hardly kick out a hundred families and replace them all."

"Fine. If it is so simple, you get them all to agree to that!" Jinda snapped. Who did he think he was anyway, she thought—living in the village for little more than a month and trying to change something they had been doing for hundreds of years!

"Please, Jinda, I am not saying it is simple." Ned laid his hand gently on her arm. "But I think it can be done. Other villages in other provinces have done it. Why not Maekung too?"

"What about other villages and Maekung?" a voice spoke up behind them.

Jinda snatched her arm away from Ned's touch and spun around. Her father was standing on the path, looking annoyed.

"We were talking about the rent, sir," Ned answered, standing up and moving away from Jinda. "Several other headmen in other villages have already decided to resist," Ned said. "In Pitsanuloke and Lampang provinces especially. In fact, so many villages are holding back two thirds of their rice crop that the rent resistance movement is growing very strong."

61

"Yes, and more and more village leaders have been arrested, or even killed, because of it," Inthorn said.

"Rumors . . ." Ned began.

"Nai Pruk of Doisaket was gunned down last week," Inthorn said. Jinda could hear the pain in her father's voice. "He was my cousin."

"I'm sorry," Ned said. "But that is one man."

"I could name you a dozen others, but I am sure you know of them too."

"Some things are not easily won," Ned argued. "Some things must be fought for."

The older man sighed. "Only people who have not lost a fight," he said, "can talk of fighting so easily."

"That's not true, sir," Ned replied. "It is people who are afraid of taking a risk who are afraid to fight."

"Well, the risk is too great, then," Inthorn said. "If we lose, we could lose our land, our crop, our homes—even our lives."

"But think of what you would gain, sir, if you won," Ned insisted.

"What? A handful or two of rice?"

"No, a better diet, healthier children, a brighter future."

"Words," Inthorn snorted. "Dreams."

Ned started to argue, but the farmer cut him off. "There's no sense talking about this," Inthorn said. "I came down here to talk to my son anyway." He looked at Pinit sternly. "I heard about Lung Tong's fence. That buffalo of yours must have his nose drilled—"

"No!" Pinit cried.

"Tomorrow morning," Inthorn said. "And I don't want to hear another word about it."

Pinit splashed over to the riverbank and wrapped his arms around his father's waist. "Please, Pa, I promise not to race him again. I promise he will be good and—"

"Stop whining," Inthorn said. "That buffalo has gotten too unruly, Pinit, and you know it. Only after we thread a rope through his nostril will he follow you meekly. That's the only way to break his fighting spirit."

"Interesting," Ned commented drily. "Does it work for peasants too? Have the landlords gotten ropes through all their tenant farmers' noses?"

Inthorn glared at Ned. "That's enough," he said sharply. He pried Pinit away from his waist and said more gently, "Don't cry, son. Come, I'll whittle a new drill to do it with. It won't hurt your buffalo too much."

"It . . . it won't?"

Inthorn ruffled his son's hair. "You can sand and polish the drill yourself. Make sure it's smooth and sharp so it'll go through easily. The animal won't feel a thing."

Jinda knew her father was lying. She had seen enough nose drillings to know that the poor animals snorted with pain and fright as the wooden drill pierced through their nostrils. And once the rope was threaded through, the animal must feel a twinge of pain in his nostrils

63

every time his rope was tugged. Glancing from Pinit's forlorn little face to the placid young buffalo, Jinda felt sorry for both of them.

She watched as her brother led the buffalo out of the water and walked him back onto the path home. Ned trailed a few steps behind, waiting for her to follow.

But Jinda hung back, feeling the need to be alone. It was dusk, and the shadows around her were lengthening. In the distance the mountain ridge curved in a wide arc, encircling their valley. It was the most peaceful time of the day, yet all this talk of rent resistance and nose drilling, of fighting and losing, had made her uneasy.

In the twilight, a flock of skylarks were winging their way across the sunstreaked sky. As she watched them disappear, Jinda said a silent prayer for the safety of her home and family.

Several curious villagers gathered by the gate of Jinda's house early the next morning, waiting for the nose drilling. Jongrak and Ned were among those who stood by the mango tree as Pinit led his young buffalo toward them.

"Do you really have to do this, Father?" Pinit asked as Inthorn slipped a muzzle over the buffalo's head.

"I'm afraid so, child. It's the only way to tame it. A buffalo has to be made to serve his master."

"Just like a man," Ned said gravely, careful to address only the little boy.

Inthorn glowered at Ned. Grimly he tied a rope to

one end of a heavy bamboo pole and stuck the other end deep into the soil at the base of the mango tree. As he led the buffalo into the space between the tree and the pole, Nai Tong pulled the rope tight around the tree trunk until the buffalo's head was held fast.

The buffalo strained against the pole. His eyes bulged, and he breathed so hard that white froth collected on his muzzle.

Without ceremony, Inthorn put one hand on the buffalo's muzzle, then started pushing the drill into one of his nostrils.

Pinit whimpered.

The animal pawed the ground furiously, his eyes terrified. He tried to jerk free, but his head was held fast. Blood trickled out of the nostril, staining the sand.

Pinit was crying now, great round teardrops zigzagging down his cheeks. Inthorn glanced at him, then, wincing, plunged the drill through the wall between the animal's nostrils. Just at that moment, Pinit wailed.

Startled, Inthorn jabbed down with such force that the wooden drill pierced the nostril wall and plunged into his free hand.

There was a scream. Inthorn doubled over, clutching his hand. Jinda caught a glimpse of the drill as it dropped beside him. It was stained a deep red.

She ran to her father and tried to support him. To her horror, she saw that his hand was pierced through.

His thumb dangled helplessly. Inthorn was staring at the wound. His breath came in short pants.

Jinda dropped down beside her father and supported him as he slumped against her. "Get Sri," she gasped. "Hurry!"

"No, get Mau Chom!" someone in the crowd shouted. The voice was Dao's.

After what seemed an eternity, Jinda saw the onlookers parting for someone. Jinda thought with relief that it was Sri.

But the young medical student did not appear. Instead, a plump old man in a dirty singlet pushed his way through the crowd. With a sinking feeling in her stomach, Jinda realized it was Mau Chom.

Inthorn was lying half propped by the mango tree and half supported by Jinda. Reluctantly, she held out her father's hand for the spirit doctor to examine. The bleeding had eased some, but the gash was jagged and deep.

Mau Chom looked at the cut in distaste. Then, sitting back on his heels and rocking himself rhythmically, he muttered a low chant over the thumb. At the same time, he uncorked a bottle he had brought with him. The strong smell of home-brewed rice wine wafted out and he sniffed it appreciatively. Then, with a flourish, he tilted his head far back and poured the wine into his mouth. There was a brief gurgle as the liquid rushed through the bottleneck. He gulped several times, then leaned over and spat the last mouthful over the cut hand.

Jinda turned away, feeling sick. A mixture of brownish wine, saliva, and blood dribbled down her father's hand.

"Carry him home. Put him near the family altar and make sure his head points east," Mau Chom said. "I'll check on him tomorrow."

News of their headman's accident spread quickly throughout Maekung. Neighbors streamed in to visit, bringing medicinal herbs or broth. Like moths around an oil lamp, they stayed to hover around Inthorn. They were waiting, Jinda realized, not just for news of his condition, but for his advice. After all, Dusit was supposed to be coming to collect the rent in a few days, and Inthorn had not told anyone yet whether he had decided to pay less than the customary rent. Without his decision, the villagers remained undecided themselves. And so they gathered, talking among themselves in hushed tones, waiting for their leader to get better and advise them.

But Inthorn did not get better. The next day he became feverish, and that night he was completely delirious.

Jinda kept watch anxiously. Dao was there too, whether on Mau Chom's instructions or on her own initiative, Jinda did not know.

Several times during the night, Inthorn flung off his

thin blanket and struggled to sit up. Jinda and Dao tried to restrain him, but he only struggled all the more. He tossed incessantly, begging some invisible demon not to drill his nose. Neither the moist towels his daughters applied to his burning forehead nor their soothing whispers calmed him.

"He is getting worse," Jinda whispered shakily. "What will we do?"

"Get Mau Chom to say another chant over him," Dao said.

Jinda frowned. "The first one hasn't done much good," she said. "Maybe Sri should look at him. She has medicine, and—"

"No!" Dao said fiercely. "Mau Chom said that if anyone else tries to heal Father, his spell won't work. Especially Sri. She is a witch. Isn't it enough that she killed my little Oi? You want her to kill Father too?"

"But Oi was desperately sick," Jinda argued. "There is still hope for Father if we ask Sri to—"

"No!" Dao said, and she sounded so vehement that Jinda did not protest again.

The next day, Mau Chom entered the sickroom without even taking his shoes off at the door. He glanced at Inthorn moaning in the corner. Fanning himself with a sheaf of rice paper painted over with hex signs, Mau Chom nodded approvingly.

"Windows shut good and tight," he observed, "and he is pointed the right direction."

69

"But his head is terribly hot," Dao whispered.

"That is to be expected. Evil spirits are battling good spirits. That makes for a lot of heat. I will say my most powerful chant for him. It is his only hope."

Jinda frowned and knelt beside her father protectively.

Mau Chom sucked in his paunch, knelt down beside Inthorn's head, and passed his hands over the farmer several times. He began to chant in a low monotone.

In the middle of the ritual, Jinda noticed that Sri had crept in and was watching the spirit doctor intently.

When Mau Chom finished, Dao thanked him. "Will he get better now?" she asked.

"It is hard to say. I may have to say another chant or two."

"And then . . . then will he get well?" Dao asked nervously.

Mau Chom shrugged. "Sometimes the evil spirits win, despite my spells. I cannot heal everyone, you know."

Hearing this, Jinda remembered how their mother had died, wide-eyed and burning with fever after Pinit was born. Mau Chom's chants hadn't worked then, either. Jinda could no longer keep silent. "Maybe we could have Sri look at Father," she said. "I mean, she is a doctor too. It can't hurt to have—"

Mau Chom swung around and glared at Jinda. "How dare you compare that little fraud to me?" he demanded. "She is no doctor!"

From the doorway, Sri spoke up. "True, I am only a medical student now," she said quietly. "But in another year I will be a doctor."

Startled, Mau Chom squinted up at Sri. "Don't you dare touch my patient," he snapped, "or my spells will be broken."

"Your spells can't be much good if they can be broken so easily," Sri shot back. "In fact, you have done more harm than good already, spitting that mouthful of germs onto the wound."

"Germs?" Mau Chom glared at her. "It was sacred rice liquor."

"All right, the alcohol is a disinfectant, but your bacteria counteracted that."

"Go ahead, little miss witch doctor. Roll out your magic words," the older man sneered. "But if you so much as touch one hair of this man's head, he will die." With that, he got up and stomped out of the room.

The three girls looked at one another in silence. Then Dao said, "You heard him, Sri. Go away."

"But your father's hand is badly infected. He should have some antibiotics and that wound should be treated. . . ."

"He doesn't need your medicine," Dao replied.

Sri turned to Jinda. "Talk to your sister," she begged.

71

"Make her listen. You have worked with me at the clinic. You know how many people I've helped."

"I know," Dao snapped. "I know how you 'helped' my little Oi."

"Your baby never had a chance, Dao. But there is still hope for your father."

"I said go away," Dao repeated, her voice hard.

Sri shook her head helplessly. Then she left without another word.

That night, Inthorn's fever climbed. He shivered violently and stared glassy-eyed at his family without recognizing them. Jinda and Dao continued to take turns watching over him.

After the second temple gong sounded, Jinda relieved an exhausted Dao and took up her vigil. Watching her father trembling with fever, too weak even to moan, Jinda remembered how similar her mother had looked before she died. She wondered if Sri's medicine might not have saved her mother when Mau Chom's spells proved useless.

A light flickering in the doorway interrupted her thoughts. She looked up and saw Sri, her glasses glinting in the light of the oil lamp she was holding.

For a moment Jinda hesitated. Dao had gone back to Mau Chom's house for the night, and her grandmother and brother were sleeping peacefully in the other room. Jinda took a deep breath and motioned for Sri to come in.

The medical student crept into the room and knelt down beside Inthorn. She reached for the farmer's bandaged hand and turned it over. Carefully, she started peeling away the rag. Dried pus had formed a thick yellow scab around his cut and was now stuck to the cloth. The thumb was horribly swollen and the whole hand red and puffy. As Sri pulled the last shred of bandage away, the scab tore and a stream of new pus trickled out. It smelled putrid.

"Good Lord," Sri breathed. With gentle fingers she probed Inthorn's arm, his wrist, and finally his thumb. Inthorn moaned and feebly tried to twist away.

"It's pretty bad," Sri said without looking up. "The infection is spreading. It might even develop into gangrene, once it gets into the bloodstream."

"Can you cure him?" Jinda asked.

Sri looked up then, her face grim in the moonlight. "I can try," she said.

Jinda nodded. "Then try!" she said.

Sri flashed her a rare smile. "That's the spirit!" she said. "Now get me some water—boiled water. And I need more light."

Jinda lit an oil lamp and turned the wick up high. Then she brought the kettle of boiled drinking water that Sri always used.

Together they knelt over Inthorn. As Jinda held his hand firmly, Sri washed it clean with warm water, swabbing the wound with white cotton. It took a long time, but at last they could see the abscess that had formed beneath the sealed wound.

From a small bag Sri had brought with her, she now produced a thin knife and held it over the flame of the oil lamp. "Now. Hold onto his hand. Tight," Sri ordered. Then, with quick precision, she cut along the original tear. Immediately a ribbon of pus spurted out, and a trickle of blood followed. Sri heaved a sigh of relief.

"You can let go of his hand now," Sri said softly. Only then did Jinda realize that she was still gripping her father's hand with all her strength, even though Inthorn had responded with nothing more than a weak tug.

Sri washed Inthorn's hand clean, then poured a clear liquid onto the wound. White foam bubbled up. "What is that?" Jinda wondered aloud.

"Just some hydrogen peroxide," Sri said. "A cleaning solution." She kept squeezing on more of the liquid until the foaming stopped.

The cut was starkly revealed now. Deep and jagged, it stretched from one side of Inthorn's thumb clear to the other. The gaping flesh revealed the bone of the thumb below. Sri examined the wound carefully. Then she took out a small packet of black thread and a curved needle. "I wish I had some anesthetic," she breathed.

Jinda held her father's thumb in place as Sri proceeded to stitch along the cut. Each time her curved needle jabbed through his skin, Inthorn flinched. Sri was sweating now, small beads running down her cheek and collecting on her chin. She was careful to have them drop away from the wound.

There were eleven stitches in all, running crookedly across Inthorn's palm. "I wouldn't have made a very good seamstress," Sri said wryly. She applied some more disinfectant over the cut, then wrapped the whole hand loosely in gauze.

Inthorn's moans had subsided, but his face was drenched with sweat and the pillow under his head was soaked through. He mumbled inarticulately, then fell into a deep sleep.

"He will rest better now," Sri said to Jinda. "Give him these two pills every four hours. And let him sleep as much as he wants."

Rolling down the wick in the lamp, Jinda realized that her hands were trembling violently. She smiled shakily at Sri. "Thank you," she said.

"Thank you," Sri said, "for trusting me."

After Sri left, Jinda sat watching her father for a long time. He slept more peacefully, his breathing even and regular.

A night owl hooted in the distance and a passing breeze rustled the palm fronds out in the yard. Jinda felt a twinge of sadness. If Sri had been in Maekung when her mother was sick, Jinda thought, things might

75

have been different. She shook her head to clear the depressing thought away. At least her father would get well.

At dawn, just after the fifth temple gong, Inthorn stirred. In a hoarse whisper, he asked for some water. Jinda lifted a ladle of well water to his lips and slipped in the two pills that Sri had prescribed. Still dazed, Inthorn hardly noticed swallowing the pills and drifted back to sleep.

He slept for most of that day. By evening, he was restless and hungry.

"What's for dinner?" he asked weakly. Jinda, barely able to contain her tears of relief, rushed to the little kitchen and prepared a special meal for him.

Within minutes she was back, bearing a tray of food so carefully arranged that anyone would think it was an offering to the monks. There was lemongrass soup, and a sliver of salted fish over a mound of rice, and a bowl of boiled peanuts the neighbors had bought. As an afterthought, she had decorated the tray with a hibiscus in full bloom.

"Here, Father," Jinda said, placing the tray on a low round table in front of him. "You haven't eaten for days, you know."

Inthorn wetted his lips. He reached for the peanuts, then grimaced with pain. For the first time he noticed the neat white bandage of gauze swathing his hand. "I hurt myself . . . how?" he asked.

76

"Pinit's buffalo, Father," Jinda said. "You were drilling his nose when—"

"Drilling his nose," Inthorn repeated slowly, as if he were trying to remember the details of a disturbing dream. "So it really happened. I thought somehow it was my nose . . ." He looked at his daughter and smiled. "What strange dreams I have had, Jinda."

Jinda smiled back, thrilled simply because he had recognized her and called her by name.

"And all this white gauze," he asked, studying his hand. "Who did this? I remember Mau Chom . . ."

"No, Father, Mau Chom didn't do this. He only chanted spells."

"Who did this, then?"

"Sri did, Father."

"Sri?" Inthorn frowned. "She is just a young girl. Is her magic really stronger than Mau Chom's?"

"You have seen her work at the clinic, Father. She is good."

"Yes, but that was only for small ailments. I always thought Mau Chom was more powerful for the sicknesses of life and death."

"Apparently not, Father," Jinda said gently. "Sri's magic is powerful too. She cured you when Mau Chom couldn't."

Jinda took out the little packet Sri had left with her and poured the capsules out into her hand. White and red, they gleamed in her palm like wet pebbles. "See,

77

Father? She gave you this medicine for the fever. You have taken six already, and it is time to take two more. Go on, take two. Her medicine worked so far."

Inthorn looked at the capsules, frowning. "What is it?" he asked.

Tetracycline—Jinda remembered the lilting name Sri had used for those capsules when she had prescribed them at the clinic. "Tetracycline," she said softly to her father, then smiled. "Magic," she amended.

Her father smiled back at her. Meekly, he picked up two capsules and swallowed them.

Even though Inthorn was past danger, Jinda guarded him fiercely for the next two days, anxious that he should rest in quiet. Dao hovered around, offering to bring Mau Chom in to say another chant, but Jinda said sweetly that Mau Chom's chant had worked so well that another would not be needed. The matter was not brought up again.

It was not so easy, however, to keep the farmers at bay. As word got around that Inthorn was recovering, more and more villagers gathered in the clearing under the veranda, waiting patiently to see their headman.

At first Jinda, backed by her grandmother, allowed only Inthorn's closest friends up to visit. Lung Teep, Nai Tong, and Sakorn climbed the stairs quietly and sat in a little row outside the bedroom door, carrying on a hushed conversation with Inthorn while every-

78

one else sat downstairs and strained to listen. They desperately wanted to know if Inthorn, their head-man, would keep two thirds of the rice from the fields he rented and whether they should follow his ex-ample.

After three more days of being confined, Inthorn grew increasingly restless. He wanted to see how the threshing was getting on, he told Jinda. He needed to be in the fields with the rest of the villagers.

Jinda begged him to rest for another few days, but now there was no restraining him. Ignoring her pleas, Inthorn got up very slowly and started to walk down the village lane toward his fields. Her first im-pulse was to run after him and bring him back, but something about the resolute set of his shoulders stopped her.

As he walked on, neighbors and friends joined him. By the time he reached the threshing ground at the edge of his field, a small crowd had gathered around him.

Jinda hurried after him. Among the dozens of peo-ple there were Ned and Sri and, as she approached, Mau Chom and Dao arrived. This was the first time Inthorn had set foot outside his house since his acci-dent, and the villagers were curious to know what he was about to do.

Slowly, Inthorn squatted down by the mound of rice grain that had been threshed from his two plots of rice. As if oblivious to the people pressed around him, he scooped up a handful of rice and let the unhusked brown grain trickle through his fingers.

"Fifty years now," he said to no one in particular, "I have grown rice in these fields. And for fifty years, I have seen half of my crop carried off."

He looked up at the fields that stretched out before him, dry and stubbled in the sun. "I know every inch of these fields. I have plowed them and planted them, weeded them and fertilized them, harvested them and reaped the rice grain from them. I think of them as mine." His eyes lost their dreamy look and he scanned the faces of the people around him. "Brother Teep," he addressed his closest friend. "Your eight *rai* of land, do you think of them as yours?"

Lung Teep nodded.

"And Nai Tong, your land, do you think of it as yours?"

The second farmer nodded.

One by one, Inthorn turned to each of the farmers and asked the same question. And one by one, each answered in the same way.

"Well," Inthorn said finally. "It is not. That land out there belongs not to us but to some man who has never even held a crumb of soil between his fingers. A man who takes half of what we harvest, year after year." Inthorn let another handful of grain trickle through his fingers. Then he took a deep breath.

"Why?" he asked. "Why should we give him so much, when we don't have enough to feed ourselves and our children? Why are we so timid, so stupid, so tame?"

He looked at Pinit, who stood at the edge of the crowd next to his buffalo. Inthorn gestured for his son to bring the buffalo over to him. With the hemp rope strung through his tender nostrils, the once spirited animal now obeyed every little tug of the rope and meekly followed Pinit over to Inthorn. Inthorn patted the animal thoughtfully.

"Ned implied once that I was like a buffalo being led by my nose by the landlord, not daring to resist the high rent. Remember, Ned?"

The young student looked acutely embarrassed. "It . . . it was very rude of me, sir," he stammered. "I had no right to speak like that."

Inthorn laughed. "Well, what you said was right, son. I have been like a buffalo all these years, placidly obeying my master every time he tugged at my rope." He drew himself straighter, and his glance swept past the people around him. "But no more. I am not a tamed buffalo. I am a man. I can choose what to do with my life. And this year, I choose not to pay the usual high rent."

A deep sigh, as strong as a gust of monsoon wind over the wild plumed grass, swept through the group. Jinda heard it and felt a surge of pride in her father.

Not only had he just taken a major step for himself, but he had also convinced the other farmers to take the same step.

Impulsively, Jinda walked over to Inthorn and grasped his good hand. His fingers were thick and gnarled, and she squeezed them tight. When she released his hand, she saw that there were a few grains of rice sticking to her palm, passed to her by her father.

S E V E N

The villagers of Maekung talked of nothing but the rent for the next few days. Most of the farmers joined Inthorn in his vow to resist, but a few held back, apprehensive and uncertain. Suppose, they argued, the landlord or his agent, Dusit, forced them off the land? Suppose the police came and arrested them all? Suppose the students were really Communists who had come to stir up trouble in their peaceful village?

It was no coincidence that the farmers who feared these possibilities most were the ones closest to Mau Chom. He was one of the few villagers in Maekung who owned his own land and never had to pay rent, but that did not stop him from urging others to pay the customary amount.

Jinda listened to the heated discussions taking place all around her, but she was not caught up in the sense of mounting excitement. Instead, what concerned her more deeply was Dao's growing aloofness from her family. Especially as more and more villagers backed Inthorn's decision, Dao seemed to grow colder and more withdrawn.

Dao did not come home to visit anymore, nor did she ever invite her sister to visit her at her father-in-law's house. At first Jinda thought this was because Dao had aligned herself with Mau Chom against their father and was therefore avoiding her family. But gradually Jinda sensed that her sister's self-imposed isolation stemmed from more personal reasons. Dao acted moody and strangely guilty, avoiding any contact with her family and friends. Whenever Jinda managed to corner her in the village, Dao would withdraw into a sullen silence, then seize the first chance to stalk off alone.

After some time, Jinda stopped trying to go after Dao. If Dao were in any real trouble, Jinda decided, she would come to her in good time. And so, although Jinda continued to feel uneasy over Dao's strange behavior, she resolved to go about her own business as usual.

Thus, Jinda was not even thinking about her sister when she stumbled on the reason for Dao's strange behavior. One afternoon Jinda was looking for newly sprouted bamboo shoots along a bend in the river near the village. She was searching through a pile of fallen bamboo leaves when she saw a flash of red moving behind the bushes on the opposite bank.

She thought it was a squirrel at first. Then a figure moved into view. It was Dao. She had on her best sarong, its white lotus flowers printed against a gay red background. Her hair was tied back with a string of jasmine buds. Her face was clean and smooth, and she was even smiling a little. Jinda was pleasantly surprised to see how pretty her sister was. She looked as fresh and lively as when her husband, Ghan, was courting her.

Jinda watched as Dao walked along the opposite bank. Careful to sidestep the thorny mimosa bushes, Dao cast furtive glances over her shoulder, as if she were afraid she was being watched.

Near a large willow tree with trailing branches, Dao paused and called out softly. The overhanging branches parted and a man stepped out. Even from a distance, Jinda could see that he was tall, broad-shouldered, and solidly built. Dressed stylishly in city clothes and shiny leather city shoes, his face remained in shadow, so that Jinda could not tell who he was.

The man stretched out a hand and tried to pull Dao to him. Dao slapped him lightly and laughed, the high, melodious sound echoing across the river. Jinda realized incredulously that her sister was flirting. This was a different Dao, far removed from the moody, arrogant sister she had seen these last few weeks.

The man said something in a low, gruff voice, and Dao laughed again. Jinda was mystified. Who was Dao with? Had Ghan come back to her after all?

Then the man reached out an arm and pulled Dao toward him again. This time she did not resist. Still laughing, she disappeared behind the screen of willow branches.

Jinda caught a glimpse of the man's face, his teeth flashing in the dappled sunlight. No, it was not Ghan.

Jinda stared at the trailing leaves but could see no more. She did hear quiet murmurs, which were at first low and serious before giving way to Dao's breathless giggles.

For a long time Jinda watched the willows. Everything was still now. Only the dreary hum of cicadas and the occasional wail of a wild gibbon broke the silence.

Finally the delicate branches parted, and the man stepped into view. In that brief instant Jinda thought he looked familiar. Then, without looking behind him, the man walked up the riverbank and onto the hillside behind it.

Only then did Dao emerge from behind the same branches. She looked flushed and disheveled. Her hair was in disarray, the string of jasmine buds untied. Dao lifted her arms to refasten the jasmine garland around her hair, and at that moment she caught sight of Jinda. She froze, arms raised high, and gasped.

"Jinda! What are you doing here?" she said.

Jinda smiled weakly. "Collecting bamboo shoots," she said.

"How . . . how long have you been here?"

"Not long," Jinda said. "I just got here."

"You are lying!" Dao cried. "You saw us!"

"No, I didn't," Jinda said, realizing too late that her denial was an admission of guilt.

Clumsily, Dao splashed across the shallow streambed and confronted Jinda. Her face was contorted with anger and a trace of fear. "It isn't what you think, sister," she said, gripping Jinda's arm so tightly it hurt. "Dusit and I were just talking."

"Dusit," Jinda echoed, and her heart sank. Of course he looked familiar. Although she saw him only twice a year, Jinda knew the rent collector's smooth, pale face only too well. "What are you doing with Dusit?"

"Mau Chom made me go see him," Dao said petulantly. "When he saw how Father and the other farmers were planning not to pay the full rent, he made me go tell Mr. Dusit."

"And then?"

Dao tucked a stray wisp of hair behind her ear. "And then nothing, sister," she said. "I told Mr. Dusit and we got to talking, and we found we got along together very well." She glanced at Jinda and added primly, "I enjoy his company."

"You have seen him often, then," Jinda said. "In secret." She suddenly understood why her sister had been acting so strangely. "Why didn't you tell me, Dao?"

"How could I? Practically everybody in the village except Mau Chom hates Mr. Dusit. Father would kill me if he knew Dusit and I were friends. You all think of Mr. Dusit as a horrible man, but you don't really know him, Jinda. He can be very kind and charming." Dao brushed back a strand of hair from her eyes, and Jinda saw a flash of gold on Dao's fingers.

Deftly Jinda caught her sister's hand and looked at the gleaming new ring on her finger. "And this—this is part of Mr. Dusit's kindness and charm?" she asked angrily. "How can you do this to us, Dao?"

"I am not doing anything to you," Dao snapped. "This is between Mr. Dusit and me. We have grown very fond of each other. Mr. Dusit said just now that he loves me—"

"Dusit loves you?" Jinda echoed incredulously. "He takes away half of our rice, so that your own baby didn't have enough to eat, and he says he loves you?"

Dao turned away abruptly. "You don't understand!" she cried, her eyes brimming with tears. "You are just being mean and childish. What would you know about love, anyway?" She dropped Jinda's arm and ran off, her long hair streaming behind her.

A single jasmine bud dropped from her tangled hair and fell to the ground. Jinda picked it up and smelled it. Its fragrance was already gone and its wilted white petals edged with brown.

Dusit made his appearance in the village three days later. His arrival took no one by surprise, since everyone had been expecting him for weeks now. Besides, Jinda had confided in her father that Dao had become very friendly with the rent collector, only to realize that he already knew of it but had chosen to express his disapproval with a grim silence. In fact, Jinda saw now that Dao was acting aloof not of her own choice but in reaction to the villagers' whispered gossiping over her friendship with the rent collector.

When Dusit's truck came roaring down the mountain path, Jinda saw Dao slip away. Surprised, she stopped her sister and asked, "Where are you going? Aren't you going to meet him?"

"What for?" Dao demanded. "So the whole village can gawk at us and laugh?" She turned abruptly and stalked off.

Everyone else in the village, however, flocked to the threshing ground to await Dusit's truck. Within minutes, a big crowd of people had gathered there.

Soon the blue truck careened into the village, swerving so sharply that a few children had to jump into the ditch. It pulled to a grinding stop just short of the threshing ground.

Dusit opened the door and swung down to the running board. He looked relaxed yet commanding as he leaned against his truck. His clothes were bright and new, and in his sunglasses he looked like a man on one of those huge posters Jinda had seen in town advertising the latest movie. Jinda's eyes were drawn to his shiny belt buckle, which gleamed in the sunlight. No wonder Dao found him attractive.

Dusit propped his sunglasses rakishly over his forehead and surveyed the crowd. "Well, well, well," he said genially, to no one in particular. "Here I am again. As regular as the bullfrogs after the rains." He laughed, and a gold tooth sparkled in the sun.

No one spoke.

Pushing aside the farmers who stood nearest him, he made his way to the threshing ground. There he slowly circled the mounds of rice. "Pretty poor harvest," he said to Inthorn in mock friendliness. "You haven't stashed a few bushels away for safekeeping, have you?" He laughed softly, as if he were sharing a secret joke with Inthorn.

No one laughed with him.

Dusit shrugged. "All right, let's get on with it then. Let's see. There are no fertilizer or plowing costs advanced in the village, so the crop should be divided half and half as usual. Come on, let's get moving. I haven't got all day." He nodded to his assistant and the man obligingly propped a board against the back of the truck, making a gangplank to the ground.

Silently, Nai Tong lifted a bushel basket of rice, walked up the plank, and poured the rice into the empty truck. The sound of the rice hitting metal was like a sudden burst of rain. Then Lung Wan hoisted another basket of rice and headed silently across the road to the village granary, a wattle bin built on stilts high off the ground.

Inthorn was next. He lifted a third basket, balanced it between his strong neck and hands, and started walking. Slowly and deliberately, he passed the blue truck and crossed the road to the granary.

"Hey! You! Come back with that! It's the third basket!" Dusit shouted after him.

Inthorn kept walking.

Dusit flushed with anger. "Somebody stop that fool! He'll get the order all confused. That's my basket!"

No one moved. In complete silence the villagers stood watching Inthorn pour the rice into the community bin.

When Inthorn came back to the threshing ground, Dusit knocked the empty basket out of his hands. "What is the matter with you?" he demanded. "You know the first basket is mine, the second is yours, and the third is mine again!"

"Not anymore," Inthorn answered. "From now on we pay a lower rent: one basket for you and two for us."

"Who says?"

"I do," Inthorn said quietly.

"Are you crazy? Who are you to tell me what the rent is? You are just a farmer!"

"Yes, I am a farmer," Inthorn said, drawing himself

91

up very straight. "I plow the land. I sow the seed. I transplant the seedlings. I water and weed the fields. I harvest and thresh and winnow. Why shouldn't I also have a say as to what the rent is?"

Dusit was speechless. Bright patches of purple mottled his cheeks and stained his neck and ears. "You . . . you can't do this!" he finally spluttered.

"Watch us," Inthorn said.

He nodded to three farmers, who immediately filled up their baskets. One walked to the truck, while the other two headed for the rice bin.

The division of the rice went quickly and smoothly after that. For the first time, it seemed to Jinda that the farmers carried out the task with a song in their hearts. "Watch us," Inthorn had said. Watch us, watch us, watch us. Bare feet slapped lightly on the path, bringing basket after basket of rice to the village granary.

By late afternoon, the farmers had finished dividing the rice and the threshing ground was bare. The blue truck had space for more rice, but the village granary was fuller than it had been for many years.

Inthorn hoisted the last basket of rice and poured it into the back of the truck as Dusit stood by glowering.

The rent collector was sweating heavily, his shirt soaked through. His lips were pursed in a straight, grim line. He reached out and grabbed Inthorn's arm. "You!

You are the headman of this village, aren't you?" he demanded.

Inthorn nodded.

"You're going to be in trouble, I'm warning you. Big trouble."

The farmer smiled. "With more rice than we've ever had in our rice barns? I don't call that big trouble." He shook Dusit's hand off his arm and walked away.

Dusit's face contorted with rage. He aimed a vicious kick at a mangy dog lying in his way and climbed into his truck. As he slammed the door shut, the expression of naked hatred on his face frightened Jinda. Then the truck roared to life, churning up a cloud of dust as it rolled away.

"We did it," Inthorn whispered. He looked at the guarded faces of the farmers around him and seemed unsure what to do next. Suddenly Pinit burst out into a loud cheer and clapped his hands.

It was as if a spell were broken. Inthorn grabbed his son and swung him high into the air as the villagers laughed and cheered.

"We did it!" Inthorn shouted exuberantly. "We really did it!"

That night, the whole village celebrated.

Girls threaded jasmine buds in their hair. Even Jinda's grandmother playfully tucked a bright red hibiscus into her bun. Fresh offerings of rice and flowers were placed on the altars of the spirit houses, and a new sash of homespun cotton was tied around the trunk of the old sacred rain tree. A bonfire was built near the rain tree, and a few of the less scrawny chickens were killed to make a big pot of chicken curry.

Nai Tong and his brother brought out their long drum, and Lung Kam played his three-stringed lute. Ned and the students, who were nowhere to be seen during Dusit's visit, joined the celebration. Late into the night, the villagers danced to their simple music, weaving upturned palms in the traditional *ramwong* dance.

Jinda danced with Vichien and other village boys, but out of the corner of her eye she kept watching Ned. He clearly had become the village hero. He was either surrounded by giggling girls or in a quiet corner conferring with the men. Jinda watched him become the center of attention as he moved from one group to another.

Suddenly, he was standing beside Jinda. "I'm not very good at dancing," he said, "but maybe you could teach me."

Eyes glowing, Jinda led the way to the circle of light where couples were dancing. Trying very hard to keep her smile demure, she began to move to the rhythm of the music. Ned followed. As they danced around the fire, their bare arms traced sinuous patterns in the

94

air. They never once touched, but Jinda was acutely aware of his nearness.

"You are very beautiful tonight, Jinda," he murmured as they circled each other.

Jinda's cheeks burned. The fire seemed suddenly too bright. She danced away from it, and Ned followed. As they wove their way past the other dancers, their fingertips touched. Ned held on to Jinda's hand briefly. She felt strangely excited and calm at the same time.

The glow of the fire stroked Ned's face with light and shadows. Jinda wished her fingertips were like the firelight, long and feathery and playful on his cheeks and throat.

The drumming slowed and the music from the lute trailed away. Jinda and Ned stopped dancing and separated, but not before Ned's hand brushed against hers one last time.

As Jinda left the bonfire the cool night air caressed her face. She felt a surge of happiness so strong that she wanted to burst out laughing.

Then she saw Dao. Standing under the rain tree, she looked very lovely, and very alone. A single jasmine blossom, white against her black hair, glowed in the firelight. Dao hadn't danced all evening. The villagers had avoided her, as if she already belonged to Dusit. Jinda walked over to her sister, but Dao turned and disappeared into the night.

*   *   *

The mood of celebration did not last long. Within two days Dusit was back again in Maekung.

This time he parked his truck right next to Inthorn's house. A stranger wearing a khaki uniform was in the seat next to him. A police officer. Jinda watched from the gate as the two men got out of the truck.

"Is this the village headman's house?" the policeman asked.

"I am the headman," Inthorn said. He had been sawing a teak log to replace some rotten planks on the veranda, and he carried his saw with him as he stepped forward.

Dusit eyed the saw nervously. "Put that thing down," he said.

Smiling, the farmer did so.

"So you are the man who plotted to resist paying the rent?" the policeman asked him.

"There was no plot," Inthorn replied calmly. "Every man made the decision for himself." Nai Tong and several farmers had gathered by the truck to listen. A few of them nodded their heads in agreement.

"That is beside the point," Dusit said. "As the headman, you are responsible for the villagers. Many here refused to pay the full rent and so," Dusit paused and smiled grimly, "I am having you arrested." He nodded to the police officer, who stepped toward Inthorn.

"Wait!" Ned pushed his way through the crowd and

96

stood between Inthorn and the policeman. "You can't arrest him," he said. "Headman Inthorn has not broken any law."

"The hell he hasn't! He didn't pay his rent!"

"He paid one third of his harvest yield. That is not breaking the rent law."

"What do you know about the rent law?" Dusit demanded. "I have been collecting rent since before you were weaned, you pup! I know when someone hasn't paid his legal rent."

"No, you don't," Ned said evenly. In his calm, clear voice, he told Dusit that the new government was considering passing a new law limiting the rent to one third of the crop. "Until this proposal is either passed or rejected," Ned said, "there is no legal rent. Paying half of the crop is only traditional, not a legal arrangement. And therefore headman Inthorn has broken no law."

Dusit listened, open-mouthed. Beads of sweat were glistening on his forehead, and he flicked them off. "How do you know all this?" he asked.

"Does that matter?" Ned countered. "The point is that the law does not stipulate that a tenant farmer's rent is half of his crop."

The policeman frowned. "Who are you?" he asked abruptly. "You don't talk like a peasant. You sound more like some Communist trained in Laos or Vietnam."

"I am as Thai as you are," Ned said.

"Commies consider themselves Thai," the policeman said. "Even though they take their orders from Vietnam."

"I am not a Communist," Ned said.

Dusit eyed him skeptically. "So who are you?"

For a second Ned hesitated. "I am a student," he finally said, "from Thammasart University."

The policeman and Dusit exchanged a quick look. "I thought so," the officer said. And, although he sounded hostile, his voice held a grudging respect.

Withdrawing to the truck, the two men conferred in low voices. "I can't arrest that Inthorn now," the police officer said quietly. "Not with a Thammasart student watching. He is right. Refusing to pay the traditional rent is not illegal."

"Then arrest him for some other reason!" Dusit snapped. "These peasants are always breaking some law or other."

Suddenly Dusit smiled. He sauntered over to the log that Inthorn had been sawing. "Looks like a good solid log you have here," he said with studied casualness. "Teak, right?"

Inthorn nodded warily.

"Cut it yourself?"

Again Inthorn nodded.

"Where did you cut it from?"

Inthorn hesitated. He looked uncertainly at Ned. But Ned looked puzzled too.

"You got it in the Suthep mountains, didn't you?" Dusit asked pleasantly. "Where most of the teak trees have already been cut?"

"Yes, but I cut down only one log," Inthorn protested. "Those mountains were stripped bare by the timber company."

"Oh, I know that," Dusit said. "The timber company has a concession to cut those trees. You don't." His voice became harsh. "You broke the law when you cut that teak tree down." He nodded at the police officer. "That's illegal timbering, isn't it? Go ahead then, arrest him."

There was stunned silence. It had all happened so fast that no one could do anything.

Dusit laughed at Ned. "Want to consult your Thammasart textbooks about that, son?" he said. "I have not been to your fancy university, but I know one thing. Illegal timbering can get a man up to fifteen years in prison."

"Fifteen years!" The whisper reverberated through the crowd.

Inthorn looked around desperately. The policeman stepped forward and grasped his arm.

"No!" Inthorn cried, wrenching free. The next moment he turned and dashed through the crowd.

The villagers parted to let him through. Jinda saw him plunge out of the crowd and to the fields beyond.

Run, Father, run, she urged him silently. Faster!

And then a shot rang out.

The policeman had dashed after Inthorn, waving a pistol in the air. "Stop or I'll shoot again," he cried.

But Inthorn only ran faster. He sprinted toward the stubbled fields and the river, where he would be safe in the thick underbrush. Run, Jinda urged him in her heart. Run, run!

There was a second shot.

Then utter silence.

Inthorn crumpled in a far corner of the field. Jinda saw him sink slowly to his knees, a small black dot among the brown. For what seemed an endless moment, he did not move. Then Jinda saw him straighten up very slowly.

"Thanks be to Buddha," Jinda breathed. The soft prayer of relief echoed through the crowd. "Thanks, thanks be to the Buddha."

The police officer ran to Inthorn and took him by the elbow. Inthorn shook him off. Alone, head held high, he walked unsteadily back toward the stunned crowd. Jinda saw that the hand injured by the bullock was bleeding.

Looking dazed, Inthorn allowed the policeman to steer him into the truck.

When he was seated, Jinda approached and gently examined his hand. The new wound did not look serious. The bullet had just grazed the back of his hand, and the stitches on his palm were intact. Carefully Jinda poured some water over the wound, rinsing off the dirt and blood. Pinit handed her another ladleful

100

of water, and she used that too. When the graze was reasonably clean, she looked around for something to use as a bandage.

Pinit understood. Quickly he stripped off his T-shirt and handed it to his sister. She wrapped their father's hand in it, knotting the sleeves together. It made a loose, clumsy bandage, but at least it would keep the dust off during the long ride ahead.

E I G H T

In the month that Inthorn had spent in prison, no one had been allowed to visit him. Jinda had tried especially hard to see him, but without success. Together with Ned, she had made the long trip into town several times, petitioning for permission to see Inthorn. But each time they were passed from one official to another. It was only because Ned was educated and from Bangkok that they got to see anyone at all. Medical treatment? Sorry, but a doctor was called in only in exceptional cases. Visits? Sorry, but orders from higher up stipulated that Inthorn Boonrueng's case was special, and no visitors were allowed. Bail? Sorry, he didn't qualify for it. An early trial? Sorry, but there was a backlog of cases awaiting trial and he would have to wait his turn.

The waiting seemed interminable. Then at last, when she was on the verge of giving up, Jinda received a letter from the prison authorities informing her that she could visit her father.

She held the precious letter in her hands as she sat in the oxcart on her way into town. On her lap, under the letter, Jinda held a cloth bundle containing home-made coconut patties and a package of medicine that Sri said would help if his hand had become infected. Jinda hugged both the letter and the cloth bundle to her.

In the morning light, the paved road stretched out ahead of the oxcart, shiny as new lacquer. Patches of dew glistened like shattered glass on the weeds along-side the road.

The team of oxen ambled on, their wooden bells clanking melodically. It was still chilly. Jinda edged her toes over to a patch of sunlight on the wooden cart and wiggled them. Ned slid his foot over and gently nudged Jinda's toes with his own. Jinda looked up and smiled at him. If nothing else, she thought, at least Father's arrest had brought her closer to the Tham-masart student.

The two of them sat close together, so that with each sway of the cart their shoulders bumped to-gether. Each time they touched, Jinda felt the warmth of Ned's breath on her neck, and this both comforted and excited her.

Jinda wished that Dao was with them too. But her sister had moved out of Maekung not long after In-thorn was arrested and had not contacted her family since. There were rumors that she was living in town, perhaps even with Dusit. Jinda sighed. She felt bad that Dao had felt so ostracized by the villagers that she had left Maekung altogether.

"What are you thinking about?" Ned asked her now.

Jinda started guiltily. It was really no use brooding about Dao now. "Nothing much," she told Ned. "What a lovely morning it is!" She smiled at him, and the warm smile he returned her dispelled her gloomy thoughts.

The sun was high in the sky by the time their ox-cart arrived at the prison. It was on the outskirts of town, and at first sight, it seemed more of a carnival than a prison. Makeshift stalls set under bright sun umbrellas dotted the square. People milled about, clutching children and shopping baskets behind them. Except for the tall stone walls looming behind the gay umbrellas, it could have been any marketplace.

Under their striped canopies, wooden stalls held piles of fried chicken and sticky rice. Jinda paused by a mound of tangerines and eyed them wistfully. Her father was very fond of tangerines. If only she could afford to buy him some! But Ned steered her past the fruit to a booth right in front of the prison gates.

This was where visitors registered their names. Carefully, Jinda wrote her name in a ledger. The officer who manned the booth looked at her with interest.

"Jinda Boonrueng," he read aloud. "Are you In-thorn's daughter?"

Jinda nodded.

"He is a special case. Allowed only one visit and needs special permission for even that. Have you got permission?"

Jinda produced the letter and held her breath.

The man in the booth nodded. "All right," he said. "Only this once, and only two visitors," he said.

Left to wander around, Jinda listened idly to the snatches of conversation in the market. A few of the people there were farmers, but most were residents of the town. A plump woman with long, blood-red fingernails was complaining that the police had closed her husband's gambling den again. Two pock-marked teen-agers were comparing the price of heroin.

"Hear it's getting more crowded than ever," one of the teen-agers said, nodding toward the prison.

"That's hard to believe. Packed twenty-eight men to a cell when I was in. Couldn't turn over at night without waking the guy next to you."

"Well, at least you were never in the Blackhouse," the first boy said. "I was shut up there for a week once. No windows, no light, no toilet. Pure hell, that's what it was. When I came out the sunlight was so bright I couldn't see for hours."

Despite the warmth of the noon sun, Jinda shivered, wondering how her father had been treated these last four weeks.

There was a sudden crackling sound, and the crowd grew quiet as the metallic voice boomed out of the loudspeaker strung up above the market.

"Group Twelve," the voice announced. "Visitors to the following inmates can now proceed inside the prison. Single file at the gate, please."

A list of names was read out. When the voice announced Inthorn Boonrueng, Jinda and Ned started walking toward the prison gates. There uniformed guards ushered them through a narrow doorway in the prison wall. Ned took Jinda's hand as they stumbled along through a dim corridor to an equally dim but much bigger room.

The room was partitioned into three sections by iron bars, the middle section empty except for two prison guards. Sandwiching the prison guards were the visitors on one side of the iron bars and the prisoners on the other side. There were about six feet between the two groups. Jinda had only a second to take this in. She was shoved by the crowd toward the iron grill and had to fight blindly for a space next to the bars. A little boy wriggled past her, squeezed himself between her and Ned, and clung tightly to the bars.

At first Jinda could not see her father. Separated by the gap, the men on the far side of the partition looked dark and indistinct. Then Ned shouted "Inthorn, sir! Over here! Here!"

Desperately, Jinda scanned the faces of the caged men. At last she found her father.

He had aged. In the dim light his face looked haggard and sallow, and long lines tugged down the corners of his mouth. His clothes hung loosely on him. One bare shoulder, thin and smooth, protruded from his torn shirt.

Around his ankles were iron shackles.

Jinda stared at the shackles in horror. Thick iron bands were clamped around each ankle, linked together by a thick chain. He was the only prisoner with shackles. Could a farmer be considered more a menace than heroin pushers and gamblers?

Inthorn shuffled toward them, the shackles clanking as he moved. In his hands he held part of the chain, lifting it as he dragged each foot along. He carefully edged his way until he was directly in front of them. Jinda saw that he was trying to say something but the noise of the others shouting drowned his voice.

Clutching the metal bars, he mouthed the same words over and over. Only by watching his lips move could Jinda make out what he was saying. "Get me out," he said. "Get me out!"

"We are trying," Ned shouted above the tumult. "I'm going back to Bangkok soon; I'll organize some protest marches—circulate a petition . . ."

Inthorn shook his head. "Hurry," he called out. "My hand . . . it's getting bad." He looked extremely tired. "Please hurry," he cried.

Already a bell was shrilling. Guards pried visitors away from the bars. Many clung on, screaming last messages at the men on the other side. A few thrust bags of food and cigarettes at the guards, who grudgingly ferried them across to the prisoners. Jinda, too, shoved her parcel of food and medicine at a guard, begging him to pass it on to her father.

"What is in it?" the guard demanded, taking the parcel.

"Coconut cakes," Jinda said. Then, seeing that he was unwrapping it anyway, she added, "And some medicine."

The guard pulled out the package of blue-and-white pills. "Sorry, drugs are contraband," he said.

"But it is for my father's hand!" Jinda protested. "He is hurt!"

The guard shrugged. "Rules are rules," he said, pocketing the pills. He sauntered across to the other partition and handed the parcel over to Inthorn.

"Father!" Jinda called to him.

Inthorn took the parcel and looked up at Jinda. For the first time during the visit, he smiled. "Jinda," he called, stretching out his arms to her through the gaps in the bars. Only then did Jinda see that his left hand was swollen and bloodstained. The T-shirt bandage she had wrapped around his wrist was in shreds.

"Father, your medicine!" Jinda shouted.

"Medicine?" he echoed faintly, looking relieved. "Good, thank Sri—"

"No, Father, they took—"

But a guard was pulling her father away, dragging

him by his chains through a narrow doorway on the other side of the visitation room. Jinda, teeth clenched to stop the tears, leaned her head against the bars. The metal felt cold and smooth against her forehead.

Someone gently pulled her away from the bars and for a brief moment she found herself in Ned's arms. Choking back her sobs, she clung to him as they walked down the dark corridor outside.

The sunlight seemed glaring when they emerged from the prison gates. Jinda blinked away her tears and took some deep breaths. When she had composed herself, Jinda turned to Ned. "He looks so weak," she said. "Did you see his ankles? They are scraped raw. And his hand needs medical attention, or he . . . he . . ." She paused and looked uncertainly at Ned.

"Or he may die," Ned finished. He said it so matter-of-factly that Jinda felt a surge of frustration and rage.

"No! How can you say that? He's sick, yes, but he is still a strong man!"

"Jinda, let's face it," Ned said. "Your father won't be able to stand it in there much longer."

"If he dies, it will be all your fault," Jinda said, feeling on the verge of hysteria. "You, with your talk about resisting the rent. You got Father in there," Jinda insisted, her voice growing louder. "Now you have to get him out!"

"I understand how you feel, Jinda," Ned said quietly. "I am going to try my very hardest to have him released. As I tried to tell Inthorn just now, I plan to leave for Bangkok soon. I can organize a movement to free him once I'm back there."

Jinda swallowed hard. Ned was leaving? But how could he desert her just when she needed him most? She felt angry and betrayed but did not know how to express it.

"The sooner I get back to Bangkok, the sooner I can get to work on this," Ned said. "I will need time to build Inthorn into a powerful political symbol of feudal oppression."

Those words hit Jinda like a slap in the face. Was that what she and her father and Maekung meant to Ned? Were they all just "symbols of feudal oppression"?

"Leave! Go ahead, leave!" Jinda cried. "The sooner the better!"

For the next week, Jinda kept her distance from the students. She found out that the universities in Bangkok were about to start the new semester, and she couldn't help thinking that Maekung had just been a vacation for them. Now that the vacation was over, it was time for the good little students to go back to school.

Jinda's hostility did not really include Sri, Jongrak, or Pat; it was directed at Ned. The strength of her emotions scared her, and she tried to keep them in

110

check. Still, she felt betrayed by Ned, by the keen interest he had taken in her before her father's arrest and his gentle concern afterward.

But she wondered now whether Ned had only pretended to like her. She thought back to the times he had waited for her after Sri's clinic and of the long walks home they had afterward. She thought of how he helped fetch water from the well and emptied her buckets into the earthenware jars on the veranda. And he had been wonderful to Pinit and their grandmother, too, helping the boy wash his buffalo and splitting kindling for the old woman. Jinda had come to think of Ned as a close and dependable friend.

Yet it seemed obvious to her now that this was not the case. She and her family were but political symbols that the students had used for their own purposes. If Ned thought of her father as "a symbol of oppressed farmers," he must think of her as a "simple oppressed peasant girl" and not as Jinda, a young woman attractive and appealing in her own right. Humiliated, Jinda felt hurt and betrayed.

In the days before the students' departure, whenever Ned tried to approach her, Jinda would turn away and pointedly avoid him.

Finally, on his last evening in the village, Ned stood stubbornly outside her gate and waited for her. Jinda's grandmother noticed him as she was sweeping the veranda.

"What are you doing, just standing there?" she called to him.

"I was hoping to talk to your granddaughter," Ned replied.

"Well, come up then," she said with a laugh. "I'll get her."

By the time Ned climbed the stairs, the old woman and a sullen Jinda were waiting for him on the veranda.

Jinda's grandmother motioned to Ned to sit down next to her. "So you're leaving," she began. "When are you coming back?"

Jinda's pulse quickened. She had never dared to ask that question herself. For once, she was glad her grandmother was so blunt.

"I don't know," Ned said. He turned and looked at Jinda. "But I do hope to come back soon."

"Well, I hope so too. You are a good boy, even if you do have some strange ideas." The old woman was silent for a moment. "You have managed to change more things in this village in a few months than anybody has in my whole lifetime! I trust that these changes will turn out well even if there is trouble now. In the meantime, since you are leaving us, I want to give you a proper farewell." Carefully, she picked up a thick strand of homespun cotton and held out her hand to Ned.

"Give me your hand," Jinda's grandmother demanded. "The left one."

Ned obediently stretched out his left hand.

Rocking gently from side to side, the old woman murmured a long blessing, her voice undulating with the same rhythm as her rocking. It was the traditional leave-taking ceremony of the North. The old woman was calling back any of Ned's wayward spirits that might have strayed into the village, so that he could leave a whole man.

"Spirit of Ned's eyes, which have seen good things and bad in Maekung, come back to him," she chanted. "Spirit of Ned's ears," she continued, winding the white thread around and around his wrist, "come back to him."

When the chant was finished, Jinda's grandmother solemnly tied a knot on the thread bracelet. The strands of cotton looked very white against Ned's brown arm. "Bless you, child," she said. "And come back soon. We will miss you." She got up and slowly walked back to the kitchen.

Ned stroked his thread bracelet and looked across the veranda at Jinda. "I meant it, you know," he said quietly. "I will be back soon. I don't really want to leave. One of the reasons I am returning to Bangkok is to try and get Inthorn released from prison. Jinda, look at me. Don't you believe me?"

Jinda kept looking at her hands. "What does going to Bangkok have to do with my father?" she asked.

"You have seen how useless it has been, trying to get the officials in town to help. This whole rent question has become too controversial and too widespread for the provincial officers to handle. We have to raise the issue with the politicians in Bangkok."

Politics again, Jinda thought bitterly. Games of the city.

"I know what you must be thinking," Ned said quietly. "And I think I understand, but I want to tell you that you are wrong. Come on, Jinda, let's go for a walk. Give me a chance to explain." He looked at her earnestly. "Please, it means a lot to me."

Jinda relented, and in silence they walked down the small trail behind the village and up the adjacent hillside. Ned did not talk much, perhaps sensing that Jinda mistrusted his fluency. Instead, he pointed out many small things in Maekung that he would miss, and he tried to tell her how happy he had been in the village.

"I feel at home here, Jinda," he said. "I admit it, I came to Maekung for political reasons, to try and spread the rent-resistance movement into this area. But Maekung isn't a political issue anymore. It has become my home, too." Then, awkwardly, he told her about his own home, something that he had never mentioned before.

"I don't really have another home," he told Jinda. "I grew up in a village like this, except even poorer." During one particularly bad year, he said, after a swarm of rats devastated the rice harvest, there hadn't been enough to eat in the village. "My father went away to find work in Bangkok, and I never saw him again. The same year my mother died in childbirth. That's right,

Jinda, like yours." His hands were clenched, and Jinda wanted to smooth his fists open and stroke his palms.

"Go on," she said.

"There isn't much else to tell," Ned said. "I was sent to live as a temple boy in a local monastery, where I stayed until I was sixteen. I was a pretty good student—there wasn't much else to do except study—and I got a scholarship to attend a high school in Bangkok, and then another scholarship for Thammasart University." He talked of the drab, cluttered rooms he had occupied in Bangkok and of the long days spent in classes and meetings. He smiled apologetically at Jinda. "It's no wonder that I talk like a book sometimes. I haven't known much else. And," he paused and sighed, "sometimes it's easier to talk like a book than a person."

"I like it better when you don't talk like a book," Jinda said quietly.

Ned reached out and took her hands in his. "And me? Do you like me?"

Jinda said nothing, but she left her hand in his. They had walked to a mango tree in the far corner of the yard, near the little spirit house. There Ned put his hands on her shoulders and drew her close. Jinda could see the beating of his pulse at the base of his throat.

"I want you to promise me something," Ned said softly.

"What?"

"Come to Bangkok soon," he said.

115

"Why?" Jinda asked.

Ned hesitated. "I plan to organize a rally about the high rent soon, and you could be a very effective speaker at it," he said.

Jinda stiffened. "There are others who can give speeches better than I," she said. "You don't need me in Bangkok for that."

"You're right," Ned admitted. He swallowed hard and looked distinctly uncomfortable. "Let me try again," he said. "Jinda, please come to Bangkok soon, because I want to see you again."

Jinda felt a sudden lift of her spirits. She looked up at him and smiled. "Now that," she said, "is a much better reason."

He pulled her to him and gently held her against him. For a giddy moment, she felt the hardness of his chest and the heat radiating beneath his thin shirt. Then he pulled away and took a deep breath.

There was an amaranth bush growing nearby, and he bent down and picked a single blossom from it. He held the small purple flower out to Jinda. "Do you promise, then, to come to Bangkok soon—to see me?"

Jinda took the flower from him. "I promise," she said.

Ned smiled, a sudden boyish grin that lit up his whole face. Then he turned and walked away. Jinda watched him pause by the little spirit house and quickly bow his head toward it, just once. Then he was out the gate and walking down the dusty little trail, his white shirt billowing in the evening breeze.

The air was cool and fresh, and the sun was just setting. A single shaft of light illuminated the spirit house. It looked unkempt and forlorn, its wooden walls warped and its roof sagging.

Jinda went over to it and hesitated. Then she stood on tiptoe and dusted the altar with a square of banana leaf. She placed the amaranth blossom Ned had just given her on the altar. There was no incense or fruit or any other offering there.

She remembered the day her father had built the spirit house, sawing the little pieces of wood and carefully fitting them together. Her mother, her grandmother, her sister, and Jinda herself had all stood around, admiring his workmanship. When he had finished, they had helped place fresh offerings on it until it brimmed with fruits and flowers. How full and happy it had looked then!

And how empty, how terribly empty, the little structure seemed now. Slowly, without bowing, Jinda turned and walked away.

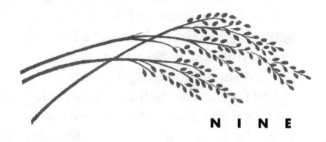

The days passed very slowly after the students left Maekung. There was little for Jinda to do, no one to talk with, and nothing to look forward to. Nor was it just Ned's absence. With both Inthorn and Dao gone, Jinda's grandmother and little brother seemed lost and disheartened. The old woman spent hours sitting at her loom, her hands lying idle on her lap, while a subdued Pinit played nearby.

The Maekung villagers tried to comfort Jinda's family. Several farmers took over the tasks that Inthorn had done before he was imprisoned. When the July rains came, Lung Teep and Nai Tong came to plow

118

and harrow Inthorn's fields, and later other villagers helped to transplant the tender rice seedlings. Jinda was grateful for their help but uneasy that she couldn't reciprocate.

"Don't worry about that," Lung Teep assured her with forced cheerfulness. "Inthorn can always help plow our fields when he gets out." But both he and Jinda knew that would only happen in the distant future, if indeed at all. Inthorn had not been allowed permission for another visit, despite several attempts on Jinda's part to see him again.

The one bright spot in Jinda's life was the steady stream of letters from Ned. Eagerly she awaited the postman's visits as he puttered into their village on a rusty motorcycle.

When Ned's first letter came, dozens of villagers crowded around as Jinda tore open the envelope. Knowing that she was expected to read it aloud to them, she felt relieved rather than disappointed that the letter was quite impersonal.

In his letter, Ned described the hectic organizing that he had become involved in as soon as they got back to Bangkok: the printing and distributing of leaflets, the protest marches, the petitions, the numerous articles in the newspapers focusing on tenant farmers of Thailand. All this activity seemed rather remote to Jinda, but out of loyalty to Ned, she willed herself to believe that it was crucial in working toward her father's release.

119

Toward mid-August, Ned wrote that a big demonstration against the high land rent was scheduled to be held in early October and that he hoped Jinda could come down to Bangkok to help plan and speak at the rally.

It was only in a postscript that he had added cryptically, "It's important that you come soon to help organize this rally. But come for that other reason too." Jinda smiled, reading that.

When Jinda broached the subject of going to Bangkok to her grandmother, however, the old woman frowned.

"Bangkok is so far away," she protested. "How will you get there?"

Jinda showed her the train ticket that Ned had enclosed with his letter. Jinda's grandmother squinted at the ticket dubiously. "Even if this little bit of paper will get you to Bangkok," she said, "where will you stay once you're there? It's a huge place, and we have no relatives there."

Jinda handed her another piece of paper tucked inside Ned's letter. "This is a map to Sri's house," Jinda explained. "Sri wrote asking me to stay at her house while in Bangkok."

Her grandmother shook her head. "Your young man seems to have thought of everything," she conceded. "You're quite determined to go, aren't you?" She looked up at Jinda, and there was a tired sadness in her eyes that Jinda had never seen before.

Jinda hesitated. "It won't be for long, Granny," she said gently.

"That's what your sister said when she left. That was three months ago, and I haven't heard a word from her since."

"Well, we've heard that she's living with Dusit," Jinda said. "She knows we won't approve of that, so she probably feels it's better to keep her distance. But I'm not Dao, Granny. I will stay in touch, and I really will come back soon."

"So many of you have left me," the old woman murmured, as if she hadn't heard Jinda. "Baby Oi, Inthorn, Dao, and now you." She paused, then reached over and touched Jinda's cheek lightly. "But don't feel bad, Jinda. Leave if you must. I will still have little Pinit."

Jinda smiled. "And I will be back soon," she promised. "I really will."

"I know you will, child," her grandmother replied. "And I will be here waiting for you when you return. In a strong wind, the spores of a fern scatter, but when the wind dies down, there will always be spores that take root around the old fern, and there is new growth again. Someday soon, we will be a real family again."

She got up and flexed her knees. "Now help me get some of my homespun cotton," she said briskly. "I want to say my farewell blessing for you."

* * *

Jinda touched the bracelet of twisted white thread on her wrist now, as she settled back in her seat on the train. The thread felt soft and comfortingly familiar.

Then she felt the train start with a small jerk. Up ahead, its whistle blew piercingly as the engine slowly picked up speed. On the platform outside, boys balanced trays of boiled peanuts and coconut cakes as they trotted alongside the train, trying to make one last sale. Standing a little away from them, knots of people waved good-bye to the passengers.

Jinda settled back into her seat. No one was sending her off, and she had no money to buy snacks with. As the train moved out of the station, she watched the vendors, the platform, and finally the station itself recede into the distance.

Soon they were out in the countryside. The rice fields stretched out in both directions, burnished a gold-green by the late-afternoon sun. The western range of the Doi Suthep Mountains had slid past now, and Jinda thought she could see the familiar hilltop where she had sometimes watched the train snake its way between the valleys. She could imagine Pinit standing there now, his small hands shading his eyes from the slanting rays of the sun, as he watched the train go by.

The thought made her sad, and Jinda turned away from the window. She looked around her. Her section of the train was packed full. Passengers were crammed four-deep into the seats. Others perched on armrests, and some even curled up on newspapers in the aisle.

A young woman was sitting next to Jinda, hugging a plastic airline bag. Jinda glanced at her out of the corner of her eye. Her hair had been permed into frizzy curls, and she wore a blouse so sheer that Jinda could see her bra underneath it.

The girl tore open a paper bag, took out a steamed meat bun, and started eating. She noticed Jinda watching her and grinned. "Here, want one?" she asked, her mouth full of pork.

Jinda's mouth watered. The buns smelled of garlic and basil and meat. She had never accepted food from a stranger before, but then she had never been in a train before either.

"Thank you," Jinda said with a smile and she picked out a bun from the bag.

For a while they ate in companionable silence. Jinda savored each bite. The bread was chewy smooth and the filling salty and fragrant. She had seen such buns for sale but never had one before. No wonder they cost three baht each!

The girl finished eating and licked her fingertips delicately before turning to Jinda again. "Have you been to the city before?" she asked. "No? Wait till you see it. It's a great place! Some of the shops are so big it would take days just to walk through them. A whole floor selling nothing but lipstick and eye shadow and perfumes—can you imagine that?"

Jinda listened with curiosity. After her long description of Bangkok's department stores, the girl told Jinda that she was moving to Bangkok to work. She had started working in town six years ago, she said, and it was time to move on to the city.

"Don't get me wrong," she said conversationally. "I liked the place where I was working. I had regular clients who always paid in full and were hardly ever so drunk they would hit you or anything. The house-mother wasn't bad either. Of course she took half of what we earned, but she did keep the police off our backs. It was a good setup, and I sent my two brothers through school with the money I made. I really hated to leave. I wish I could just stay on there."

Jinda listened, confused. "Why are you moving, then?" she asked.

"It's the clients," the girl explained. "You know men. They get tired of seeing the same faces year after year. They say they might as well stay home with the wife if there're no new faces around. They were getting tired of me." She examined her bright red fingernails carefully. "It will be better in Bangkok anyway. I hear the pay is better, and it will be easy to find work."

Jinda was still mystified. "What sort of work do you do?" she asked shyly.

The girl raised her eyebrows. "Are you serious?" she retorted. "Come on, what do I look like—a nun?"

With a flash of comprehension, Jinda understood.

She flinched. "Sorry, I thought you were one of us," the girl said and laughed. "Here you are, a pretty young village girl, traveling down to the big city alone. What else was I to think? Don't look so shocked, sister! It's not that uncommon these days. Lots of young village girls are doing the same thing. And it's always the same story, too. Father had to sell off the land, Mother pawned her earrings, and then Daughter pitched in by selling the only thing she has to sell—her body." She glanced at Jinda and shook her head. "Shocked you again, didn't I? But it's one way to make a living. And it's better than selling off land and jewelry—after all, you can sell your body again and again. Right?"

Jinda nodded, but the bread stuck in her throat. She swallowed with difficulty, then quietly slipped the rest of the pork bun underneath her seat.

The girl had taken off her sandals and tucked her legs under her. Squirming into a comfortable position, she curled up and went to sleep.

Jinda looked out the window. There was nothing familiar about the scenery now. The mountain ranges near home had receded from view long ago. It was dusk. Sprinkled on the horizon were the flickering lights of scattered villages. Jinda felt strange seeing the darkness creep in without the sounds of crickets and bullfrogs that had always accompanied it. She felt a pang of homesickness but brushed it aside. The rhythm of the train's wheels was comforting in their regularity, and listening to that, Jinda was soon lulled to sleep.

She awoke with a start. She thought she had heard Pinit calling her, his voice shrill with excitement. Blinking, she looked up. A boy was standing in the doorway of the train, hanging precariously on the handrails as he craned his neck to look out.

It was daybreak, and most of the passengers were still asleep. Jinda climbed over the legs of the girl sleeping beside her and went lurching down the aisle toward the boy.

"Hey, get back in here," she called as she approached him. "You might fall off the train like that."

He looked back at her and grinned. "Look!" he said.

Unable to resist, Jinda leaned out too and looked.

The world outside was a beautiful patchwork of lush green. In the first rays of morning light, newly transplanted rice seedlings glowed a translucent gold. Sparkling water flowed from one paddy field to another, catching bits of sunlight. There was not a single mountain or even a hill to be seen. The fertile rice fields stretched out, absolutely flat, all the way to the horizon.

In the distance, she saw a little girl in a yellow-flowered sarong skipping on a bund across the fields, brandishing a twig at a flock of ducklings. As the train whipped past, the girl looked up and waved gaily, the ducklings splashing around her and nibbling at the clusters of duckweed.

"Now, isn't that a pretty sight?" a gruff voice said behind her.

Jinda turned and saw a man holding firmly onto the little boy's shirttail. She smiled at them both. "It's beautiful," she agreed.

"We're in the Central Plains now, nearing Bangkok," the boy's father said. "The land is certainly flatter here, and more fertile."

"I have heard they can plant two, even three crops a year here," Jinda said.

"Probably. Everything's richer near Bangkok. That's why I'm moving my family there." He gestured to a group of children nestled against a woman in a nearby seat. They were obviously from the countryside. Their clothes were faded but clean, their belongings tied up in cloth bundles.

"What are you going to do in the city?" Jinda asked.

"Why, get a job, of course," he said. "I have heard construction work pays pretty well."

"And your family?"

"My wife can work a sewing machine—she could be a seamstress, easy. And the boys can go to school, maybe all the way to high school so they can work in air-conditioned banks when they grow up. Perhaps someday we could run a small coffee shop, sell roast chicken and papaya salad . . ." There was a dreamy look in his eyes as he gazed at the lush fields sliding by. "And when we have enough money saved up, maybe we will buy a big piece of land back home."

127

"Where is home?" Jinda asked.

The farmer hesitated. "It was in Lampang. We rented six *rai* of land, but with the harvest so poor these last two years, there just wasn't enough rice to live on."

"After giving half of the crop to the landlord," Jinda added bitterly.

The farmer looked at her in surprise. "Of course," he said.

"Of course," Jinda echoed.

The train was approaching the outskirts of Bangkok now. Long lines of trucks drove by, piled high with baskets of cabbages, gunnysacks of rice, mounds of pomelos and tangerines. It seemed as if all the produce of the lush fields was being siphoned into the city.

"No wonder they call it the City of Angels," the farmer said softly, using the traditional name for Bangkok. "There is so much here, it must be like living in heaven."

The little boy ran back to his mother, shouting, "We're here! We're here!"

"Where?" his mother asked.

"The . . . the City of Angels!"

Jinda smiled.

They passed busy streets lined with storefronts. Huge glass windows displayed dresses, food, gleaming motorcycles, even sinks and toilets. Jinda grew dizzy just trying to see it all.

The other passengers in the train were stirring now. There was a sense of exhilaration as mothers hugged laughing children and men gestured at the scenes outside. A new life, the train seemed to be saying reassuringly, a new life, a good life.

Just then the train streaked past a dense, ugly section of huts. Bits of cardboard, warped planks, plastic sheets, and chicken wire were all thrown together as if a storm had pushed all the houses of a very poor village into one messy pile.

Jinda caught a glimpse of two girls squatting on a lopsided porch. They were brushing their teeth and spitting white foam into a swamp so putrid the water looked like tar. Jinda blinked several times before that cluster of huts flashed by.

Then again came wide streets teeming with cars and Jinda wondered whether she had imagined that sudden unpleasant scene. Before she had the chance to mull over her thoughts, the train was slowing down.

"Last stop, Hualumporn Station in Bangkok," a voice announced over the loudspeaker.

Jinda squeezed her way back to her seat and gathered up her bags. Then she joined the rush of passengers who pushed their way down the steps to the platform. For a moment she felt as if she had just been dropped into the middle of a swirling storm. Dozens of vendors swarmed around her waving trays of sliced watermelon, plastic toys, thick news-papers.

"Chewing gum! Cough drops! Tiger Balm! Hor-licks! Sour plums!"

"Taxi? Want a taxi, miss?"

"Headline: Singer Mali shoots lover inside Pat-pong bar!"

Clutching her bags, Jinda stumbled toward the main gate. People seemed bent on blocking her way, trying to sell her things. Passengers from the first- and sec-ond-class compartments barged by, their luggage piled onto flat carts pushed by porters. Jinda eased her way out of the mainstream of traffic and took a deep breath.

At the edge of the station platform, Jinda saw a man asleep on a bench. His wife and brood of children hud-dled on the ground around him. They looked as if they had been camping at this spot for days. Their blankets were grimy with soot, their faces blank with exhaus-tion. Jinda stared. This was no trick of the imagi-nation.

Slowly Jinda walked out the gate. On patches of lawn or around a bench just outside the station, many fam-ilies huddled together. With a sinking feeling, Jinda realized that these were farmers like the family she had just met on the train, who had come down to make a living in the City of Angels.

Jinda took a long, hard look around her. The noise and exhaust of buses and trucks were overpowering. A veil of dust and smoke hung in the air, draping the early morning sunlight with gray. On the steps of the station several children, thinner and much more ragged than her little brother, were selling garlands of wilted jasmine blossoms.

Jinda's mouth tightened into a grim line. So this was the City of Angels.

T E N

The bus ride to Sri's house was long and confusing. Twice Jinda got on the wrong bus, and each time when she asked the conductor for directions, she was acutely aware of her rural accent.

When she finally got off at the right street, Jinda was pleasantly surprised to find it so quiet. A shady lane lined with swaying casuarina trees stretched in front of her, and the air was clear and fresh.

Clutching Sri's map, Jinda walked down the lane. High walls crowned with bits of broken glass bordered the road. At regular intervals, breaking the monotony of these walls, were ornate metal gates. Behind them, Jinda caught glimpses of whitewashed mansions with tiled roofs set amid green lawns. It seemed to her that an inaccessible world of grace and beauty existed behind the walls, far away from the grimy bustle of the city.

132

The smell of curry drew her farther down the lane. She had eaten nothing except the steamed pork bun on the train. Quickening her pace, Jinda rounded the bend in the road and saw a small table laden with tureens of steaming curry. A plump woman stepped out of a side gate in the wall and set another bowl on the table.

Just then five monks in single file padded by Jinda, their bare feet silent against the asphalt. Heads bent, arms cradling round alms bowls, the monks paused by the table. The plump woman reverently ladled food into the alms bowl of the first monk as he murmured a blessing before moving aside for the next monk.

Jinda edged closer, marveling at the generous helpings of eggplant curry and steaming white rice ladled out into the monks' alms bowls. She knew the people in this house must be earning a lot of spiritual merit, offering so much food to monks. Peeking through the iron grill of the gate, Jinda saw a huge mansion with marble columns. It was far more palatial than anything she had yet seen that morning.

The last of the monks had passed by with downcast eyes. Jinda inched toward the food-laden table. Mounds of rice were still piled on one platter. The bowl of curry was barely half gone. Jinda swallowed hard. Her stomach was churning, her mouth watering at the smell of the curry. She stood to one side and cleared her throat.

133

The plump woman ignored her and started packing away the offerings. When she clamped a lid onto the pot of curry, Jinda coughed again, more loudly.

"Yes? What do you want?" the woman said irritably, finally acknowledging Jinda.

"I . . . I wonder if you could help me find the house I'm looking for," Jinda said humbly. She glanced at the note in her hand. "It is Number Twenty-five, Prathipat Road."

"You've found it," the woman said, pointing to the number on a gleaming name plate on the gate. "This is the house."

Jinda shook her head. "There must be some mistake. I am looking for a . . . a regular house. Where Sri Pramatinodh lives?"

The plump woman lifted her eyebrows. "You know Sri Pramatinodh?" she asked skeptically.

"Yes," Jinda said. Hesitantly, she held out Sri's letter to the other woman, but it was brushed aside impatiently.

"All right, show that to the mistress," she said. Her eyes swept over Jinda quickly. "The agency is sending them younger and greener, it seems. You haven't been in the city long, have you?"

"I arrived this morning," Jinda answered politely.

The woman shook her head, sighing. "Well, we do need somebody pretty badly. I suppose you will do. Both housemaids have just quit and Madame is having an important tea party this morning." She packed up the trays on the table and nudged the metal gate open with her foot. "Come on in, and bring the rice with you. Might as well start making yourself useful."

Jinda followed her through the gate and into a huge garden shaded by large tamarind and frangipani trees. Rose bushes bordered the vast lawn and, as Jinda walked past them, she felt as if she were being swept away by the scent of the flowers.

The house at the end of the curved driveway looked even more impressive up close. In fact, it seemed more like a grand temple, with its towering pillars. A flight of marble steps led up to a massive door of carved teak. Jinda had never seen anything so magnificent in her life.

The plump old woman led her past the mansion and through a shed where three gleaming cars were parked side by side. Finally they arrived at a row of neat, whitewashed rooms. So this is where Sri lives, Jinda thought. No wonder she found Maekung poor and dirty.

"Which . . . which room is Sri's?" Jinda asked.

The fat woman stared at her. "Don't be silly," she snapped. "This is the servants' quarters."

She pointed to a bench alongside one wall, where she told Jinda to wait. Then, noticing Jinda wistfully eyeing the curry, she thrust a plate of food into Jinda's hands.

"Here! If you just got here this morning, you probably didn't have any breakfast," she said gruffly.

135

Jinda stared at the food. The delicious smell of basil and peppers and fried chicken wafted up to her. For a moment she was mesmerized. She had never smelled such a rich mix of meat and spices before. Her stomach growled. She looked up guiltily.

"It is no crime to be hungry," the woman said. "Eat."

Jinda hesitated for a mere fraction of a second. Then, heart pounding, she spooned up a piece of chicken. It was delicious. Barely taking time out to breathe, she ate spoonful after spoonful of the white rice moistened with gravy.

The woman lowered herself onto the bench next to Jinda, and sighed. "It does me good to see someone eating like that," she said. "No matter what I cook, the young mistress hardly touches her food."

Jinda spotted another morsel of chicken and scooped it up.

"Not that she even eats at home much these days," the cook said. "Just a cup of tea in the mornings and not a thing until she comes back late at night." The woman mopped her head with a dish towel. "She has her mother worried sick, poor lady. It is worse than when that hairy white boyfriend came visiting Miss Sri last year, after her trip abroad. This year she spent her school break in some village up north, and . . ." She shook her head. "Like a disease, it is, but worse. Know what has hit her?" She leaned toward Jinda and whispered loudly, "Politics."

Jinda shoveled the last spoonful of rice into her

mouth and smiled. But before she could say anything, a clear, high voice called. "Noi! Noi, where are you?"

The cook jumped up with surprising speed. "Noi? Or Lek then," the voice continued. "Lek! Lek! Where are any of you?"

The back door of the mansion swung open and a tall, thin woman wrapped in a gauzy, floor-length robe stepped out. "Somboon!" she called to the cook. "Where's Noi? Or Lek?"

"Noi left your service, Madame. Last week, if you will remember."

"And the other one? Lek?"

"Yesterday afternoon," Somboon said.

"But she can't have. She knew I was having Lady Rachanee over for tea today. She must have planned this."

"You dismissed her," Somboon pointed out quietly.

"Did I? I suppose I did. Still, it was very inconsiderate of her to provoke me into firing her. What about the new maid? Wasn't she supposed to come this morning?"

"Yes, but . . ."

For the first time, the tall lady noticed Jinda. "You," she said peremptorily. "What's your name?"

"Jinda."

"Say, 'Madame'!" Somboon hissed in her ear.

"Madame," Jinda echoed obediently.

"Have you worked as a serving maid before?" she asked.

137

"No," Jinda said, then added, "Madame."

"I wish we had more time to break you in, but I suppose you will have to do for now. Somboon, see that she puts on some decent clothes and show her where the tea things are. Use the celadon set today. And serve the strawberry tarts. If the living room doesn't have fresh flowers in it, we will use the morning room."

Still talking, she walked off, the hem of her long robe sweeping after her.

"Don't look so worried," Somboon said to Jinda. "It is not all that hard. I will show you what to do."

"I don't understand," Jinda said. "Why should I do anything?"

Somboon looked frustrated. "You heard Madame. She needs you to serve tea to an important guest. Now hurry up and change. You don't have much time."

In a starched white blouse and black sarong Somboon had provided, Jinda paused at the back door to the mansion. Then, taking a deep breath, she entered the house. The marble floor was cold beneath her bare feet, and she walked behind Somboon down a maze of corridors before she found herself outside a large, airy room.

"In there," Somboon whispered, handing her a tray on which were arranged a tea set and some pastries. "And remember, stoop as you walk."

Jinda slipped into the room, balancing the tray.

"Lower!" Somboon hissed.

Jinda stooped even lower, so that she was almost doubled over. Not even when she had offered food for the village abbot had she bent this far. Why did she have to stoop so low now?

As Jinda approached the coffee table, she saw two pairs of women's legs, each neatly crossed and ending in glossy high-heeled shoes. There was a flow of soft, melodious conversation around her.

As she set the tray on the table, she remembered Somboon's hurried instructions. She was to drop to her knees at the low table, then serve tea while kneeling.

Nervously Jinda knelt beside the low table and set each teacup on it. Then she started pouring the tea. A few drops of water splashed out onto the table.

"Gently," she heard the tall lady caution, as she passed the first cup forward. A pair of bare, pale arms reached out and took it.

Jinda was too engrossed in pouring the second cup of tea to notice that someone else had just entered the room.

"Sorry to interrupt, Mother," a familiar voice said above Jinda's head.

"What is it, dear?" the tall woman answered.

"I just wanted to let you know I won't be home till late tonight. I have a meeting at Thammasart."

With a shock, Jinda realized that it was Sri speaking. Her accent and diction were so much more fluent and assured than Jinda remembered. She almost sounded like another person.

"How late will you be?" Sri's mother asked.

"Past midnight, I am afraid."

"Take your car, then."

"But Mother, please. The buses are more convenient."

"More proletarian, you mean." There was an appreciative titter from the guest. Sri's mother laughed as she said, "You see how quickly I have picked up their jargon."

"I'm late, Mother," Sri said abruptly. "See you soon."

"Wait, at least join us for a cup of tea," Sri's mother said, motioning Jinda to serve the tea to Sri. "The revolution can wait for five minutes."

Hesitantly, Jinda held out the steaming teacup to Sri. She ignored it.

"Mother, I . . . I need to go now. I d-don't want any tea." Sri's voice was tense, and Jinda heard the slight stutter that she knew so well.

"All right, dear, don't have any tea," said her mother evenly, "but you will take your car. I will not have you riding buses alone at night."

"Mother, I will n-not take the car."

"Then, Sri, you will be back tonight by nine o'clock."

"Nine o'clock!"

"That is when the women's dormitories close, isn't it? If you are not going to observe my rules, you can move right back into those awful little dorms again."

"But, Mother . . ." Sri pleaded.

"Goodbye, dear. Have a nice day at the revolution."

Sri turned away so angrily that she bumped against the low table, knocking the teacup that Jinda was holding onto the floor. Jinda gasped as the teacup smashed against the marble floor.

"Jinda!" Sri cried out in sudden recognition. She dropped to her knees next to Jinda and grasped both of Jinda's hands in her own.

"You know this girl?"

"Know her? Mother, this is Jinda. I lived with her family for two months. She is like a sister to me! And you're treating her like a servant! Come on, Jinda, get up." Sri scrambled to her feet, tugging at Jinda.

Confused, Jinda allowed herself to be pulled to her feet.

"Wait a minute," Sri's mother said. "At least pick up the broken porcelain. It is my best tea set, after all."

Jinda dropped to her knees again.

But Sri would not let go of her arm. Almost angrily, she yanked Jinda back up again. "Don't let her order you around too," Sri said vehemently. "Just because she is used to being obeyed, she thinks she can oppress every—"

"That is quite enough, Sri." Her mother's mocking tone had turned steely. "Either join us for tea or go and make your revolution. I hardly think you can do both at the same time."

"Don't worry, I am going," Sri said, pulling Jinda with her.

"And please," her mother called after her, "don't bring any more stray proletarians home, will you?"

Drawing deep, shuddering breaths, Sri sank down on the bench in the servants' kitchen. Her face was flushed a bright red, and her eyes looked suspiciously shiny. Jinda sat down beside her and squeezed her arm.

"She had no right, no right," Sri stammered tearfully, "to treat you like that. To mock you, insult you. . . ."

"She didn't know, Sri. She wasn't expecting me. She thought I was the new maid."

"But it's like this all the time, the deliberate humiliation, the mocking. . . ."

Jinda realized with a flash of insight that Sri was referring mostly to herself. She took her friend's tightly clenched fist and gently pried it open. Sri's hand was pale and smooth compared to Jinda's tanned, callused one. She patted Sri's hand gently. How strange this is, Jinda thought. Sri has everything, and I have nothing. Yet here I am, trying to comfort her.

"Don't feel bad," Jinda said soothingly. "And don't worry about me, I can always stay at Ned's."

Sri lifted her tearstained face, and Jinda wiped it with the edge of her sleeve. Just then she caught a glimpse of the cook's face, peering through the kitchen window at them. Somboon looked so shocked that Jinda couldn't help bursting out laughing.

Sri accompanied Jinda part of the way to Ned's. She was late for class and, when they came to a long, green bridge, she pointed to the other bank. "Ned lives on the other side of the river, in Thonburi," Sri said; then she hurried off in the opposite direction.

Jinda paused in the middle of the bridge to get her bearings and looked down at the water. It was clogged with rotting debris. She turned away quickly at the sight of a dead cat bobbing by, its bloated belly a hump in the water. Ned apparently lived in a very different part of Bangkok from Sri.

On the other side, Jinda passed a line of storefronts. In one window was a bald mannequin, its plastic breasts jutting out above a sequined skirt. In the shadows behind the mannequin, pale seamstresses slouched over sewing machines, their faces shrouded in swaths of paisley cloth.

Down an alley, makeshift shacks that had been tacked together from plastic sheets and corrugated metal roofing crowded together. Children darted in the tiny spaces between the houses, tossing bottle caps and mud marbles in noisy games. Jinda threaded her way through them, stepping on the zigzag of planks that served as walkways above the stagnant, mosquito-ridden swamp.

She passed by an old wooden desk under a tall banana tree. Behind it a schoolboy in uniform was bent over his textbooks, one hand stroking a plump hen nesting in the top drawer.

The little boy smiled up at Jinda as she passed. "Where are you heading, sister?" he asked conversationally. He spoke with a familiar Northern accent, and Jinda warmed to him at once.

"Looking for a friend," Jinda replied. She stopped to stroke the hen.

"I know most everybody around here."

Jinda showed him Ned's address.

"Brother Ned!" the boy exclaimed, and his smile broadened. "Everybody knows him. He's famous. His picture was all over the newspapers last year. He was even on TV once."

Jinda felt uneasy. This was the first inkling she had that he might be famous. Still, if Sri in Bangkok was so different from the Sri in Maekung, maybe Ned in Bangkok would be different too.

"He lives just down the lane here," the schoolboy was saying. "Shares a house with a few other students. My uncle is his landlord but he doesn't charge much rent, because he says Brother Ned speaks for all of us, and that is worth more than any rent money!"

Her heart beating fast, Jinda thanked the boy and walked on. As she made her way through the slum, Jinda began to feel strangely at home. She saw mothers patting white rice paste on the faces of their freshly bathed toddlers. Old men watered pots of orchids or lemongrass the way they did back in the village. Boys showered in the open air, their heads frothy with white soapsuds. Jinda realized that in this part of the city, the people were from the countryside. It was as if they had built a sprawling village in the middle of the city.

Ned's house was a small wooden structure, two-storied but so narrow that the laundry from the adjoining house protruded through its front window. Its wooden shutters creaked on rusty hinges as a breeze blew through.

Jinda heard sharp yipping cries as she approached the house. As she walked closer, she saw a pack of fifteen or more puppies crowded around a washbasin, barking and slurping. Mangy and thin, the pups all wagged their tails furiously as they fought for a place at the feeding trough. A man was busy pouring a pail of leftover food into the basin.

Jinda smiled. The scene reminded her of a time when she was much younger and enjoyed watching her father feeding piglets every evening.

Suddenly, pandemonium broke out. A large mongrel dog had barged into the crowd of puppies, trying to get at the food. The man with the slop bucket stumbled backward, nearly tripping over the big dog. It snarled and snapped at the man as the puppies howled.

Looking around, Jinda saw a stick lying nearby. Snatching it, she ran over and swung it into the dogfight, trying to break it up. She managed to pry the big dog away from the puppies.

"Grab its tail!" she shouted.

"Got it!" the man cried.

"Ned!"

"Jinda!"

Ned let go of the dog the same instant that Jinda dropped her stick. And the dogfight started all over again.

Laughing and cursing, Ned bent down and yanked the mongrel out again. Jinda chased it off and Ned calmed the puppies by pouring more slop into their washbasin.

When Ned and Jinda finally faced each other, Jinda's sarong was torn, and her hair, which she had pinned up especially carefully in anticipation of their reunion, was loose and disheveled. Ned looked even messier, his clothes and face splattered with mud.

They stared at each other and burst out laughing. Jinda laughed so hard she nearly kicked over the basin and had to be guided, stumbling and laughing, onto the porch at the front of Ned's house. The famous Brother Ned, Jinda thought with glee and relief, breaking up a dogfight!

Ned's face was lit up in a huge smile. "I wasn't sure if you were ever coming," he said. "I didn't want to be too insistent, but you never wrote. . . ."

"I did once," Jinda reminded him, "and you corrected my spelling in your next letter."

"Is that why you never wrote again? I'm so stupid sometimes. I'm sorry I offended you, Jinda."

"Never mind," she said, deciding not to tell him that she had been shamed, not offended, by his corrections.

"When did you get here?" Ned asked. "Have you been to Sri's house yet?"

"Yes," Jinda said, and she told him briefly what had happened.

"Poor Sri," he said when Jinda had finished. "She moved out of the dorms because she didn't have enough freedom, but things don't sound much better for her at home." He squeezed Jinda's hand lightly and smiled. "Well, you are very welcome to stay here, Jinda. Come on in. I'll show you where you can put your things."

Jinda hesitated, and Ned understood immediately. "Don't worry, I won't do a thing you can't tell your grandmother about!"

Laughing, Jinda relaxed and followed him into the tiny wooden house.

It was cool and dim inside. Jinda looked around her. The main room was bare except for piles of newspapers stacked high in one corner and a large desk by an open window. Tacked on the wall were large posters of strange-looking men, who seemed to glare down at her as she entered the room. Two of them were bearded, and the third was a benign-looking old man with a high forehead. Quietly Jinda spelled out their

147

names: Karl Marx, Vladimir Lenin, Mao Tse Tung. "What strange names!" she murmured.

Ned pointed to another poster tacked right above his desk. "Not this one. He's Thai." Jinda studied the face with interest. It was the face of a slender young man with wire-rimmed glasses, a cigarette dangling between his thin lips.

"Jit Pumisak," Ned said. "The first revolutionary of modern Thailand. He helped translate the writings of those other men on the wall, and he also spent years living in villages in the Northeast. He is the one who wrote the book on Thai feudalism and—" Ned stopped himself, and smiled. "Go on, tell me I'm talking like a book again," he said.

Jinda shook her head. "That's all right. It is nice just being here—" *with you,* she almost said, but bit her tongue.

"You must be tired. That long train ride, then Sri's dragon lady of a mother, and finally—"

"A dogfight!" Jinda finished for him. "You are right, I guess I would like a rest. And a bath," she added, looking at her dirty sarong and grimy feet.

Ned led her up a narrow flight of steps at the back of the house and swung open a door to a little room with an open window. "Our official guest room," he said grandly. "I keep it for students who are too tired to go home after late-night meetings. But it's all yours now. There are blankets and bedding in the corner." He paused at the door. "If you want to bathe, the

148

bathroom is downstairs on your left. Take your time, I'll wait for you."

In the little bathroom, Jinda peeled off her clothes and dipped a ladle into a large earthenware urn of water, just like the kind they had at home. She splashed the water over herself and scrubbed away the day's grime. The water was clear and chilly, and by the time she dried off and wrapped a fresh sarong around her chest, she was feeling refreshed.

She returned to the main room, where she saw Ned standing by the window, reading. It was dusk, and with the sunlight already fading, he had to squint a little. Brushing the last beads of water from her bare arms and shoulders, Jinda went over to his desk and turned on the reading lamp.

"You shouldn't read in such dim light," she said.

Ned looked up to smile at her, but his smile faded as he saw her in her sarong. Abruptly he turned his face away, so that he stood facing the poster of Karl Marx. "And you shouldn't walk around in just a sarong," he said, addressing Karl Marx. "You are not in Maekung now, and I don't think your grandmother would approve."

Jinda stared, bewildered. Then she laughed. "I thought you were talking to white-bearded Uncle Karl Marx!" she said. Then she turned and fled up the stairs into her little room.

Jinda had almost finished changing when there was a knock on her door. "What is it?" she called.

"I have a meeting in a little while," Ned said through the door. "Would you like to come?"

"Will it take very long?"

"I am afraid so," Ned said. "Probably past midnight."

"I think I'll just stay here," Jinda said. "I feel pretty tired."

"All right," Ned answered. "If you get hungry, there is some fruit downstairs."

After he left, Jinda stared at the closed door. She felt alone and a little depressed. She wished that Ned had stayed and spent her first evening in Bangkok with her. Perhaps he no longer felt as close to her as he did when he left the village. Had she come all the way to Bangkok only to find that he would be too busy to be with her? Jinda spread a rattan mat next to the window, then leaned out. The window overlooked the front door, where several of Ned's stray puppies slept, nestled together for warmth. Jinda smiled. Feeling a little like a stray herself, she pulled a cotton shawl from her bag. The shawl smelled of home, of charcoal smoke and straw.

Jinda wondered whether her grandmother was having trouble starting the cooking fire without her, and she hoped Pinit was seeing to it that the drinking jars were filled with well water. For the first time, she thought she understood a little of what her father must feel, locked up in prison and cut off from his family and the land he loved. But there was no sense brooding. She had come to Bangkok to help get her father released from prison, and brooding wouldn't do any good.

She lay down on the mat and snuggled under her cotton shawl. The noises of the street diminished as night fell, and Jinda soon dropped off to sleep.

She was awakened by a sound outside the door. Footsteps? She listened again, but the whole house was quiet. It had turned cool, and a fresh breeze blew in through the window. Jinda thought sleepily that the meeting must have broken up at last.

The door to her room swung open noiselessly, and someone tiptoed in. In the dim light from the open window, Jinda saw that it was Ned.

Her pulse quickened. Peering at him between half-closed lids, she lay very still, pretending to be asleep. He came into the room and stood over her for a moment, then knelt down by the foot of her mat.

She heard a faint thud as he set something on the floorboards. Then she saw the flare of a match. Shielding the flame with one hand, Ned bent over and lit something. Jinda saw a faint red glow, smaller than the tip of her grandmother's cigar, near her feet.

Ned edged over to Jinda. Slowly he reached out an arm toward her. Jinda held her breath. Taking care not to wake her, Ned gently lifted a corner of the shawl

151

and pulled it up over her bare arms. Then he stood up and slipped out of the room, closing the door behind him.

Jinda sat up to see what the glow by her feet was. Balanced on the neck of a Singha beer bottle was a mosquito coil, its musky incense curling up to keep the insects at bay. For a long time Jinda watched the tendrils of smoke spiraling up. So Ned still cared after all. Smiling, Jinda lay down again and closed her eyes. This time, she slept soundly until morning.

E L E V E N

The next morning Ned took Jinda across the river again, to Thammasart University. The campus teemed with students, all clutching thick books and hurrying from building to tall building. Many wore uniforms of starched white shirts and black trousers or skirts. What impressed Jinda most were the tiny metallic buttons and shiny belt buckles embossed with, Ned had explained laughingly, the name of the university. "Pure snob appeal," Ned had said, apparently by way of explaining, too, why he and most of his friends wore the dark blue work shirts and baggy trousers of farmers. Nevertheless, not a single person wore a sarong except for Jinda. She felt very old-fashioned and out of place in hers.

In class, they found seats together near the back of the room. Jinda was relieved that the desk hid her sarong. She looked around at the students, who were busily scribbling down notes. The lecturer, a small, chubby man with a mustache, brandished a piece of chalk at the students and talked about turning society upside down.

"He has just returned from America," Ned whispered to Jinda as the professor paused for breath. "He has read hundreds of books and joined massive antiwar demonstrations in Washington. He's a real progressive!"

Jinda nodded, but she was not certain she understood. She listened carefully when the professor resumed his lecture. He strung long words together so quickly, Jinda was reminded of how nimbly her cousin Mali could string garlands of jasmine buds. He spoke of fighting and violence, but he didn't look as though he would be much use in a fight. Jinda shook her head, trying to understand what his teachings had to do with her father and problems back in Maekung.

After class, Ned introduced her to a group of students standing in the corridor. "This is Inthorn Boonrueng's daughter," he said to them. "You know, Inthorn of the rent resistance movement," he added.

This seemed to excite the students. They clustered around her, asking her breathless, complicated questions. Bewildered, Jinda backed away.

"Wait a minute," Ned said, waving them aside. "Right now we have more important concerns than mere politics. Jinda and I are going to have lunch. Anyone want to join us?

"This will give you a chance to meet some of the

people you will be working with on the land reform rally," Ned told Jinda as he steered her away. "Some of them are textbook radicals. They talk a lot about revolution, but they haven't set foot outside the classroom. Don't worry. They all mean well."

Jinda glanced back at the students following them, chattering and laughing. They may mean well, she thought, but can they get my father out of prison?

In the cafeteria, Jinda stood in front of the long line of food. Tray after tray was piled high with chicken curry, vegetables, and meat. She was stunned at the sight of so much food. She stood before the tray of fish curry and another of stir-fried cabbage, torn between the two. Noticing her hesitation, Ned ladled a helping of each onto her plate of steaming rice. Jinda was overwhelmed. It was not until she had sat down that she realized everyone else had taken three, even four, different courses. Did city people eat like this every day? No wonder Ned and Sri had found her daily fare of broken rice and fish sauce so inadequate.

That evening, when Ned and Jinda got back to his house, there was already a neat semicircle of shoes around the doorstep, and a steady drone of voices reached them through the screen door.

"We're late," Ned said. "The meeting's started without us." He kicked off his sandals and went in.

Jinda remained outside, looking at the shoes. Most of them were white canvas tennis shoes, but there were pairs of leather shoes, some rubber slippers, and even one pair of shiny high heels. Slowly Jinda kicked off her own rubber sandals. She noticed that hers were worn and rust-brown with dirt—the only pair to show any sign of contact with soil.

In the next few weeks, Ned took Jinda to so many places and introduced her to so many people that her head spun. She followed him to newspaper offices where she was interviewed by reporters who noted her every word. She visited a textile factory where workers were on strike. She made the rounds of university groups active in organizing the upcoming rally. She met farmer leaders from northern and northeastern Thailand who had come to Bangkok to speak out against high land rents.

Jinda spent most of her time at the headquarters, a set of dingy rooms in a two-story building near Ned's house. There students who had been elected to represent each of the dozens of universities and vocational colleges all over Thailand gathered. They were a tight-knit network, capable of mobilizing thousands of students at a day's notice. And Ned, as one of the representatives of Thammasart University, was pivotal in this network.

At dilapidated desks piled high with leaflets, earnest-looking students incessantly banged away at old typewriters. A battered mimeograph machine cranked out leaflets with a constant soft staccato stutter. Ceil-

156

ing fans churned the still air, often swirling up a piece of paper or two.

At first Jinda could not get used to the constant whirl of noise and activity. When she was attending a discussion group on land reform, she would be distracted by a news report coming from the radio that was never switched off. Or, when she was helping to write an article about the farmers' rent movement, the contact prints that the student photographers carried out from their little darkroom always seemed more interesting.

Jinda found it hardest to concentrate during the long political meetings. She felt alternatively bewildered and bored by the talk. Her attention would wander off to the sound of the children playing in the street below, or she would watch the noodle vendor chopping green scallions in his stall. Sometimes, when she got really restless, she would water or prune the potted orchid hanging by the window. Its waxy green leaves reminded her of the thick foliage at home, and just touching them always calmed her.

Jinda liked sitting next to Sri at the meetings. She had a quiet, blunt way of asking sensitive questions that reminded Jinda of her grandmother. And often Sri would sense exactly when Jinda's impatience might peak and flash her a quick smile of sympathy, which would restore Jinda to a better mood.

As Jinda came to understand more of the political terms, and as meetings focused more on how to free her father and other farmers imprisoned for resisting

157

the rent, Jinda found herself becoming more interested and involved.

Busloads of tenant farmers were arriving from up-country and convening at the headquarters, where they joined the long discussions about rural problems. Feeling herself an integral part of such groups, Jinda shared in the mounting excitement and hope. Yet together with the hope was a growing tension. Protest marches and demonstrations were being rebuffed with increasing violence. At first there were only a few minor incidents, consisting of a few hooligans throwing rocks at the marchers. But as October approached, the incidents became uglier and more frequent. Homemade bombs had been thrown, demonstrators had been beaten up, and there were even rumors that bullets had been fired by ruffians.

The student groups had split over how to respond to this escalating violence. Two factions had emerged. The larger one, of which Ned was a key leader, argued for patience and nonviolence, while a splinter group insisted that taking up weapons for self-defense was the only realistic solution.

This was the subject of a particularly intense meeting one afternoon. Jinda sat at her favorite spot by the window underneath the hanging orchid. Sri was perched on a desk close by.

Ned called the meeting to order. "As you know," he said, "the purpose of this meeting is to discuss how to respond to the violent disruptions of our demonstrations. Yesterday smoke bombs were thrown into the midst of the protesters."

"So what?" drawled a brawny, thick-lipped student named Kamol, whom Jinda had come to dislike. "Who's afraid of a bit of smoke?"

"It's not the smoke that worries me," Ned said evenly, looking at Kamol. "Two policemen were hospitalized after the demonstration for gunshot wounds. Two policemen," Ned repeated for emphasis.

"Good!" Kamol exclaimed. "It's about time somebody besides students got hurt in these rallies." A few of the other students nodded in agreement. "We need to fight back," Kamol said.

"That's no way to fight." Sri spoke up. "Violence only creates more violence."

"Miss Pacifist can always hide in her father's mansion," Kamol taunted. "The rest of us have to deal with the bombs."

"I think Sri is right," Ned said quietly. "There are better ways to retaliate than with violence. If we start shooting, we will only give the opposition the excuse they have been waiting for to really strike out at us."

"They don't need any excuse," another student said. "There are already gangsters calling themselves the Red Boars recruited and armed by the military to disrupt our demonstrations. We have all heard rumors that they are going to launch a serious attack against us next week at the big October rally." He sounded nervous.

"That's not all," Kamol added. "Apparently the police patrolling that rally will be fully armed, not just with the usual revolvers, but with bazookas, M-16s, and submachine guns."

"It sounds dangerous," a student said. He shook his head. "Maybe the rally should be canceled."

"No!" Jinda and Ned said at the same time. He glanced at her and gave her a quick smile. Then he continued, "That would be like admitting defeat. We must continue to protest and call for changes in Thailand, and we must do so peacefully. We have already achieved a great deal by peaceful means."

"What have we achieved anyway?" Kamol challenged. "Some token reforms to keep us quiet, that's all."

"A new minimum-wage law, legal trade unions, a progressive income tax, better hospitals. And now Parliament may even change the land-rent law," Sri spoke up. "You call these token reforms?"

"Yes, I do!" Kamol insisted. "I am talking about revolution, not reform. I am talking about drastic change—about armed warfare if necessary. I am talking about—"

You are talking, Jinda said silently, like that long-winded chubby professor in Ned's class.

"I've had enough of this," Sri broke in. "Everything seems to come back to Kamol's obsession with violence. Our purpose is to help the Thai people, not to

160

provoke a civil war." She was very pale, and her voice trembled.

"You sound scared, sister," Kamol laughed. "If you want to run back home to Mama, go ahead."

Sri stood up very straight. "I am going back to the hospital," she said quietly. "At least I know I am doing something useful there. Maybe you should try to find something useful to do with yourself, Kamol." She gave him a long, hard stare, then turned and walked out of the room.

There was a long moment of silence.

Then Jinda got up and followed Sri out of the room. Behind her the discussion resumed, a few voices holding forth loudly against a background drone.

She caught up with Sri in the alley behind the headquarters building. Sri's cheeks were streaked with tears, which she hurriedly wiped away when she saw Jinda.

"I am not going back," she said.

"Nobody is asking you to," Jinda said. "I was tired of hearing Kamol talk too."

"It is so confusing, Jinda," Sri said, slowing down to keep in step with Jinda. "It seemed so simple in the beginning. We were sincere, idealistic, hardworking—and we thought we could improve Thailand if we just tried hard enough."

"It is still simple," Jinda said hesitantly. "It's people like Kamol who make it complicated."

Sri shook her head. "That's the thing," she said. "It's

161

not just Kamol," she said. "Things are changing. At first people were very supportive and excited about our ideas. Now . . ."—She shook her head again.— "now there are smoke bombs and gunfire at our demonstrations. Who are these people we brand the 'right-wing elements'? Whoever they are, they're growing stronger and more violent. Maybe Kamol is right: we have to fight force with force. But I can't, Jinda. It would be against everything I believe."

They had reached the wider street beyond the alley, and Sri paused beside a small red car. "Sometimes I wish I could just go back to Maekung and work at the little clinic in the temple courtyard," Sri said wistfully. "Things seemed simpler then, and more real."

Sri fished a set of keys out of her purse and unlocked the door of the red car. "Listen to me," she said with a dry laugh, "talking about returning to your village when I am about to drive off in a car that costs more than what your family could earn in thirty years. Maybe Kamol is right, Jinda. Maybe I am a hypocrite."

Jinda saw the plaintive look in her friend's eyes and felt a rush of affection for her. She reached over and hugged Sri lightly. Warm and bony, Sri felt like a small sparrow. "Don't fret about it, Sri," she said gently. "Granny always says there are many roads to the same shrine."

Sri smiled gratefully. "Thanks, sister, I will remem-

162

ber that," she said, and got into the car. "Do you want a ride? Are you going my way?"

Sadly Jinda shook her head. She stood on the curb and waited until Sri's car was out of sight before she turned away.

The next few days passed quickly. Large groups of tenant farmers from all over the country convened in Bangkok in preparation for the upcoming rally against high land rent. Some farmers from Maekung had also come, and glad though Jinda was to see them, she was disturbed by the news they brought. They had heard rumors, they told her, that Inthorn's health was deteriorating and that he probably could not survive much longer behind bars. More than ever, Jinda pinned her hopes for Inthorn's release on the rally, and she threw herself into helping Ned organize it.

The night before the big rally, Jinda returned home after a long meeting and found Ned at his desk. Sitting under the lamplight with his chin cupped in one hand, he was staring out the window. He looked tired and worried.

Jinda suppressed an urge to stroke away the frown on his face. Lately she had found Ned strangely distant. Although they spent virtually all their waking hours working together, they shared very few private moments. It almost seemed as though he had been deliberately avoiding being alone with her in the last few days.

Ned looked up as she approached his desk. "You should get some sleep," he said.

"I . . . I am not tired yet," Jinda replied, wanting to prolong this quiet time with him. "I thought perhaps you could help me practice my speech once more?"

Ned hesitated.

"Of course, not if you are busy, or too tired," Jinda said hastily.

Ned managed a small smile. "No," he said. "Let's do it." He rummaged through the piles of paper on his desk for the notes on the speech.

As she took the papers from him, she noticed how carefully he kept his distance from her. He held out the papers at arm's length, avoiding any contact with her fingers. Yet even when they had known each other less well, back in Maekung, he had often touched her lightly while they chatted or strolled. Jinda turned away, disappointed.

She glanced through the notes, reviewing them. It was a strong speech. They had worked on it together, weaving into it Jinda's memories of her father with the complex subject of land rent. Ned had insisted that she memorize the speech rather than rely on notes and had already spent a few sessions coaching her on her delivery.

She stood in the middle of the room and started her speech.

"Don't clasp your hands behind your back like that,"

Ned criticized. "You are not reciting a lesson in front of a classroom."

Quickly Jinda unclasped her hands. She had often wondered why people listened spellbound whenever Ned spoke. She was beginning to understand that it wasn't just what he said but how he said it. A flick of the wrist here, a pause there, a sudden unexpected smile, and his listeners were captivated.

Now, as she spoke about the drought in Maekung, she used some of the techniques he had taught her to modulate her voice and pause for effect. She spoke eloquently of the drought, of the ruthless rent collector, of her father's decision to resist paying the traditional half of his crop.

At only one point did she falter. When she started to describe Inthorn as she last saw him, standing behind the prison bars, she stammered and could not go on.

"Talk about his leg irons," Ned prompted.

"There . . . there were heavy shackles clamped to his ankles," Jinda said with an effort, her voice strained. "He looked thin and tired, as if he hadn't slept for days. His wounded hand—" Jinda swallowed hard, but the ache in her throat would not dissolve. "I can't," she whispered.

"You have got to, Jinda. The leg irons are a political symbol—"

Jinda's nerves, already frayed, snapped. "Political!" she cried. "To you everything is political! My father

165

is a man, don't you understand? He taught me to fly kites, he whittled dolls for me, he held my hand when we went on walks. Is that political? You don't give a damn about any of that. You only want me to talk . . . to talk about those leg irons. Sometimes I think you are secretly glad he has those shackles, because they make such a good symbol!"

Ned rose and walked toward her. "Jinda, you're tired," he said. "Go get some sleep."

Jinda ignored his comment. "I suppose you find me interesting only because I am political, too, like some political souvenir you brought back from your trip to the countryside!" she said furiously.

"That is not true," Ned said quietly. "I care about you."

"You care about your precious politics!" Jinda snapped, her eyes flashing. Her voice sounded loud and shrill, but she didn't care. "You wanted me here to help organize people, and after I have performed my services you think you can just dismiss me, send me back to the little village where I belong."

"All right, since you brought it up, let's talk about it," Ned said. "What *do* you want to do after the rally tomorrow?"

For a long moment Jinda looked at him, trying to find some trace of entreaty in his face. If she thought that he wanted her to stay on, she would. But Ned remained impassive.

Finally Jinda took a deep breath and said coldly, "I

166

am leaving, of course. That's what you want, isn't it? I won't be taking up any more of your valuable time. I will leave on the train right after the rally. You did send me a round-trip ticket."

"You don't have to use that ticket," Ned said. He turned away from her and stared out the window. "I sent that ticket just so you could leave whenever you wanted to. It doesn't mean I wanted you to leave."

"What . . . what do you want me to do?" Jinda whispered.

Ned continued to look out the window for some time before slowly turning around to face her. "I want you to stay," he said, his voice so low she could barely hear it.

"Are you sure?" Jinda asked.

Ned nodded. Then he frowned and shook his head. "I don't know, Jinda. If I ask you to stay, I would be selfish. After all, wouldn't you be happier back in Maekung? All those rumors about the military taking over means it could be dangerous for you here. Besides, what could I offer you if you stay? There is not much of a future for us. I cannot promise you anything."

Jinda listened in wonder at Ned's awkward, disjointed phrases, so different from his usual smooth flow of words. "You don't have to promise me anything," she said softly. "I would stay if I just knew you wanted me to."

167

"No, Jinda. That is not enough. I want something better for us. I want us to be able to build a life together."

"Why . . . why can't we?" Jinda asked. There was a wisp of hair over his forehead. She longed to gently brush it back, but she didn't dare.

"Because everything is so uncertain. If there is violence at the rally tomorrow, I could be arrested, or shot, or forced to go into hiding. I might even decide to take up arms and join the Communist guerrillas in the jungle. I can't expect you to wait for me."

"You can't expect it," Jinda said. "But I will. I will wait for you, Ned, no matter what happens tomorrow."

Ned reached out and put his hands on her shoulders. "Jinda, Jinda," he said, shaking her gently, "do you really mean that?"

She smiled. "I am not a politician. I do not know how to say things I don't mean."

Ned laughed and pulled her to him. Holding her tight, he rested his cheek on her hair. "Jinda," he murmured over and over again, "Jinda, how can I say . . . how can I say this?"

She lifted her face and looked at him. "It's easy," she said quietly. "I love you. Try it."

Ned took a deep breath. "I love you," he said. Then his face broke into a broad smile. "That was harder than any speech I have ever made!" he said.

Jinda smiled back, then rested her face against his

chest again. His shirt was cool and smooth, and Jinda could feel his heartbeat as he held her close.

A night breeze blew through the open window and the wooden shutters creaked on their rusty hinges. A headlight from some passing car pierced the darkness, then was gone. It was very quiet, very peaceful. To Jinda everything seemed wonderful. Her father would be freed soon, and then she and Ned would build a home together. After tomorrow.

Never in her life had Jinda seen so many people.
The crowd stretched from the Thammasart University gates clear across Pramane Square to the Temple
of the Emerald Buddha. Like the incoming tide of a
stormy sea, people streamed into the square, their heads
bobbing in dark waves. Easily forty thousand, Ned had
estimated earlier that morning, maybe fifty. And more
were still pouring in.

In the distance, Jinda saw a thick cordon of armed
antiriot police, their khaki uniforms incongruous under the striped canopies of the fruit vendors surrounding the square. Closer by were tight groups of street
toughs, some displaying tattoos on their bare arms,
others strutting about with hunting knives or ropes
tucked in their belts. Jinda wondered if they were the
formidable Red Boars she had heard about.

Ned came up behind her, sensing her nervousness.
"Don't worry about your speech. You will do fine,"

170

he said. To cheer her up, he pointed out a little boy in the crowd. He was, Ned explained, a shoeshine boy who attended every rally held in the Pramane Grounds and posted himself on an empty carton to mimic the speakers. The boy was standing on a carton now, waving his arms about theatrically and shouting at the top of his lungs.

"Imperialist dogs! Democracy brothers and sisters! Dictatorship! Feudalism!" he yelled enthusiastically. He made no sense, but the stream of political catchwords tumbled forth so fluently that he drew an amused crowd of onlookers, many of whom applauded and cheered him on.

"If he can do it, so can you," Ned teased Jinda. "With a bit of practice, you'll both be great orators—" Ned was interrupted by a sudden commotion.

Several toughs rammed their way through the audience surrounding the boy, yelling at him to stop.

The boy raised his voice in response and ignored them. Without warning, one of the men hurled a rock, hitting the boy on the forehead. Howling, the blood dribbling down his cheeks, the little boy jumped off his box and tried to run, but another man grabbed his collar and started pummeling him. Some bystanders tried to pull the boy away, but most stood in their places, immobilized.

In seconds, switchblades were snapped open and pointed at those who were trying to help the boy. Immediately everyone drew back, leaving the boy de-

171

fenseless. He shielded his face with his arms as the men slapped and kicked him. One of them punched him so hard he was spun reeling into the crowd. The toughs watched him go, laughing as he crawled away.

Jinda watched in horror. The whole incident took less than a minute. The hoodlums quickly melted into the crowd. A few students started to pursue them, but Ned called them back. "We have to keep the rally peaceful," he shouted. "Don't give them any excuse for violence. There are too many of them out there."

Jinda noticed that the number of antiriot police had increased so drastically that they now stood three or four deep around the entire square. Uneasy in the presence of so many policemen, the crowd became subdued.

Dark-gray storm clouds massed overhead, blocking out the sun. There was no hint of a breeze, and the air hung still and heavy. Jinda felt a strong sense of dread. Even though her father's freedom, perhaps even his life, could depend on the success of this rally, Jinda began to wish the whole rally could be called off. Something was about to happen, something terrible.

But Ned was already at the podium. His voice boomed out, amplified by dozens of loudspeakers planted across the square. Jinda was too nervous to concentrate, partly because she knew she was to speak next, but mostly because the foreboding she felt was so powerful.

172

Her heart skipped a beat as she saw a convoy of trucks driving slowly into the far end of the square. Soldiers shouldering rifles climbed out of each truck. Behind them waited a line of white ambulances, doors already swung open.

Jinda began to panic. She looked at Ned and saw that he was holding his hand out to her. With a start, she realized that he was introducing her to the crowd, inviting her to the podium. It was her turn to speak.

Unsteadily, she walked toward him. A roar of applause greeted her. She waited for it to die down before she began her speech.

"I am Jinda, daughter of Inthorn Boonrueng," she began. To her surprise she found that her voice was steady. In awe, she heard it reverberate from all corners of the square. Her words started to flow effortlessly from her, like a kite with a lovely long tail, tugging its way skyward as she held the string. She felt exhilarated and her voice grew stronger.

"My father has farmed all his life," she said, "and yet he has never had enough to eat. Why?" She paused, and in that brief silence she felt that maybe, just maybe she could help change a bit of Thailand after all. "Because he has had to pay half his harvest to the landlord. Year after year. Flood or drought."

"Commie bitch!" A shrill voice pierced the air.

Startled, Jinda stopped.

"Keep talking!" Ned hissed.

173

Taking a deep breath, Jinda continued. Before she could finish her next sentence, another obscenity was flung at her. Shaken, she tried to continue talking.

A heavy object sailed toward her and landed where the shoeshine boy had been. There was a loud explosion. Bits of dirt and glass spewed out amid billows of smoke. People screamed and started to run.

Ned grabbed the microphone and urged the crowd to be calm. "Nothing serious has happened," he announced. "A small bomb has just been tossed at us. It hasn't hurt anyone. Do not panic. I repeat, do not panic. The speech will continue."

But some students near the podium started yelling and throwing rocks in the direction of the bomb. One even lobbed a homemade bottle-bomb at the soldiers massing at the far side of the square.

"Do not retaliate!" Ned was shouting from the podium. "Calm down. Do not fight back!"

But it was too late. Soldiers were fanning out in front of the ambulances, advancing toward the center of the square, pushing the crowd forward.

There was another bomb. It landed farther away from the speaker's platform, but the explosion was deafening—and devastating. As the smoke cleared, Jinda could see that at least five students were sprawled motionless on the ground.

There was no curbing the panic that swept through the crowd after that. Screaming, flailing at one another, people tried to claw their way out of the square.

A few students, some of whom Jinda recognized as Kamol's friends, drew their pistols and brandished them, then fired wildly into the air. It was to avoid this kind of response, Jinda suddenly realized, that Ned had insisted on Kamol's remaining at the headquarters that morning.

"No!" Ned was shouting at the students now. "Stop! Don't shoot back!"

But they ignored Ned and continued to shoot in the air. Then Jinda heard a sharp staccato rattle in the distance. She saw students dropping to their knees in crumpled heaps. The soldiers were firing into the crowd.

"Dear Lord," Ned whispered. "It's happening."

"Ned! What's going on?" Jinda clutched at his hand.

He looked at her, his eyes dazed. "It's no use, Jinda. It's over. You've got to get away. Run, quick! Along the river."

"And you? What about you?"

He shook her off. "Go!" he shouted. "If you find that my house isn't safe, go to the headquarters. Hurry!" He pushed her off the platform, and she landed clumsily on the grass below. "Run, Jinda!" he shouted.

Jinda ran. She looked back only once and saw Ned standing alone on the platform, urging people to help the wounded. Then a knot of men climbed up onto the platform and struck him. He fell, and Jinda couldn't see him anymore.

She forced her way through a heaving wall of people, their sweat rubbing off on her bare arms. Their voices were shrill with fear, their eyes wild with terror.

Someone pushed past her. In his hand was a stick pierced through with a long nail. The nail scraped against her cheek and drew blood. Jinda suppressed a scream and ran on.

She reached the big tamarind tree next to the Thammasart gates, where she and Ned had often met after his classes. A body swung from the lowest branch of the tree. Jinda screamed. The corpse's face was hidden in the shadows, but Jinda could see that its throat was rubbed raw by the thick rope, and its wrists now mere stumps, dripping red. A group of men ringed the tree, jeering. The man with the nail-pierced stick shoved past them and stood under the swinging body. He lifted the stick and struck the dangling legs.

Jinda couldn't watch. She fought her way past the crowd, sobbing for breath.

A huge bonfire had been lit at the gate of the university, its tongues of flame licking at the sky. Jinda stumbled past it, trying not to look, yet looking. Splayed out, under the flames, was an outstretched arm, palm upturned, fingertips charred. A pair of broken glasses glinted on the ground nearby, reflecting the fire. Beneath the flames, a tangle of feet jutted out, some barefoot, some with scorched sandals still dangling. Someone tossed a rubber tire on top and the flames danced even higher.

Farther ahead, Jinda saw a young girl, her white

blouse stained with splotches of bright red, being shoved into an ambulance already crammed full of bodies.

Behind the ambulance was a cordon of khaki uniforms. Jinda saw a gap in the line of soldiers. She dashed through it and ran—past the soldiers, past the crowds, past the sickening smell of burned rubber and charred flesh.

Someone screamed, but Jinda didn't stop. She kept running, faster. Faster. The rattle of machine guns was farther away now.

The shady street where Jinda found herself was almost deserted. It was less noisy here, and not as smoky. A few fruit vendors squatted by their wagons, frightened and bewildered. They stared at her. It's the blood on my face, Jinda thought, and wiped at it with a shaky hand. She tripped on a basket displaying bunches of white lotus blossoms and ran on.

Down the pavement, against a red traffic light that no one heeded, and finally across the green metal bridge over the river to Ned's house, Jinda ran. Underneath the bridge, muddy waters swirled past. A body draped in a white shirt and a billowing black skirt floated past on the water. The face was hidden by a curtain of tangled hair. Jinda did not look down into the river again.

On the other side of the river was a vegetable market. Its wooden stalls were deserted now. Pyramids of eggplants and cabbages were left abandoned. Jinda slowed her pace as she came to the narrow alley that led to Ned's home. She hoped it would be safe there, but to be sure she hid behind the hedge and peered in first.

It was not safe. A jeep was parked outside and men in tight khaki pants were coming out of Ned's house, laden with boxes of papers and books. She watched as they tore down the posters of Mao Tse Tung and Karl Marx, leaving them crumpled on the floor. Then one of them switched on Ned's tape recorder.

Jinda heard her own voice, clear and plaintive, singing Ned's favorite song. "If I could be born a bird, with wings to fly, far far away, I would ask to be a dove, to lead my people in their fight for freedom." Jinda heard herself sing in a voice and in a time that now seemed incredibly remote.

She forced herself to leave the scene. She walked slowly and steadily. Don't run, she told herself. Don't panic and don't look back.

Behind her the song continued, fading ever so gradually as she walked out of the alleyway.

On the main road, the tanks were out. A line of them rumbled down the road, gun barrels jutting from gray turrets making them look like huge maimed insects groping with a single antenna. She watched them roll past.

Where could she go? Where was it safe? Then she remembered Ned telling her to go to the headquarters if his house wasn't safe.

In the distance there was a faint volley of machine-gun fire. Hearing that, Jinda felt a wave of panic. She took a deep breath, and to block out her fear, she started to count her steps. One, two, three, four, she counted, all the way down the street. She was vaguely aware of the faint gunfire behind her, but she kept walking and counting. At six hundred and forty-eight, she rounded the corner into the small alley leading to headquarters.

An unreal sense of quiet swept over her. A clothesline strung with baby clothes and sarongs flapped in the breeze. A group of boys were spinning tops on the cracked pavement.

The narrow, two-storied headquarters building stood in front of her, the front door ajar. She slipped through it.

The fluorescent lights were on, pale and cool. It was eerily quiet. The rows of desks were abandoned, the typewriters squatting mutely on them. In the far corner of the room, a small group of people huddled around a radio. They looked up as Jinda walked in. Kamol's face, tense and haggard, stared up at her.

Over the radio a metallic voice announced that the Communist plot to take over Bangkok was being crushed. "The situation is now under control. The Communists have been defeated. The Army has saved Thailand from the clutches of the Communists. Curfew is at six. Repeat, the curfew is now at six." Jinda walked over to the radio and flicked off the switch.

179

In the sudden silence, her breathing sounded desperately loud.

"Well?" Kamol asked. His eyes, ringed with circles so dark they looked like craters in his face, stared at her.

"Well what?" Jinda stared back.

"Say something!" Kamol demanded.

"What is there to say?"

"The Army. Shooting and bombs—is it really happening?"

Jinda nodded. She fixed her eyes on the potted orchid hanging by the window. "Shooting, and bombs," she repeated woodenly. A sliver of sunlight pierced one petal of the orchid blossom, making it look translucent. "And people dying."

Suddenly she was shaking, her teeth chattering. Someone gripped her shoulders and guided her to a chair. She sank into it, sitting on her hands. Her fingers felt icy cold on the back of her thighs.

"Here, drink this," someone said, pushing a bowl of hot soup toward her.

Jinda shook her head. "People dying," she stammered, clenching her teeth to keep them from chattering. A piece of pork edged with fat floated on top of the soup. Dead meat.

The retch started deep in her stomach and forced its way up. She grabbed for the bowl and threw up into it.

"Where's Ned? What's he doing?" Kamol asked brusquely. "Can we join him out there?"

Jinda put her hands over her face. "I don't know." She shook her head. "I don't know anything anymore."

"Maybe we should pack up and leave," a student said.

"Yes, if it's that bad, the police could raid this place any minute—"

Suddenly the door opened and they all jumped. Kamol was the first to recover, his laugh filled with relief. It was only Sri.

She was breathing heavily, her cheeks flushed, her short hair disheveled. Yet she seemed calm. She apparently didn't see Jinda and walked over to hand a small bag to Kamol.

"A roll of film," she said "Surat took it. He wanted it developed right away, and to have the prints sent out to the foreign news agencies."

"You saw Surat at the rally?" Kamol asked.

"At the hospital. I was treating his stomach wounds."

"Where is he now?"

"Dead," Sri said. "Please develop the film. He wanted it done immediately."

Quietly Kamol took the roll of film and went into the adjoining darkroom.

"You must all leave here as soon as possible. Remember to burn what you can't pack. I'm going back to the hospital. They are badly understaffed there." Sri headed for the door.

"Wait," one of the students called to her. "Sri, tell us. Is it really over now?"

Sri stared at the floor for a long moment. "Except for the patching up," she said finally. "God help me, except for the patching up."

She was halfway through the door when she stopped short and pulled an envelope out of her shirt pocket. "I almost forgot." she said, "Somebody give this to Jinda if you see her."

Jinda felt a sudden cramp in her stomach. "I am here," she said quietly.

Sri hesitated for a long moment before she handed the letter to Jinda. Her hand was shaking so badly she had to steady her wrist with her other hand. "Be strong, Jinda. You . . . you must be strong," she stammered, her voice barely audible.

When Jinda saw Pinit's rounded handwriting, she guessed what it was. She unfolded it. The single sheet of notepaper had been neatly ruled in pencil; Pinit's writing was neat and clear.

"Dear Sri, please tell my sister Jinda," it began, "to come home now. Our father sent word through a prison guard yesterday that he is very ill. His hand is swollen and his fever very high. Father says he cannot wait any longer for Ned's rally to help him. He only wants to see Jinda once more. He is allowed a visit. Please tell Jinda to come home first so she can take me to see Father with her. I want very much to see him before he dies. Sincerely, Pinit Boonrueng."

The room was absolutely still. It seemed as if no one were even breathing. The silence was broken by the sound of sobbing, choked and muffled. For a moment Jinda thought she was crying. Then she realized that it was Kamol, who had just come out of the darkroom. In his hands he held a sheet of contact prints, still shiny and wet.

Wordlessly, he placed it on the desk in front of Jinda and Sri. The others gathered to look.

The first photograph showed a young girl, her T-shirt pulled over her face, a knife thrust between small, slashed breasts. The second was of the bonfire in front of the Thammasart gates. Jinda noted that the glasses she had seen by the fire were crushed in the picture. The third was of rows upon rows of students made to lie face down on the ground, under raised guns held by soldiers in uniform. Jinda's vision blurred. She could not bear to look through the other pictures. But as she turned away, she caught a glimpse of the last photograph.

It was of the tamarind tree in the clearing. In the photograph, the slim corpse had swung around so its face was now out of the shadows.

Jinda saw that it was the little shoeshine boy. Blood had made jagged streaks of black on his forehead and a line of it ran down the corner of his mouth. His neck was ringed with welts, and the coarse rope pulled the skin taut under his jaw. But his stumps of wrists had stopped dripping.

Kamol was crying openly now, his broad shoulders shaking, his lips twisted into a pathetic grimace. Jinda wished she could cry like that.

She got up and walked to the window where the orchid hung. In the street below, boys were still spinning tops and the noodle vendor was still slicing scallions. Everything had changed, Jinda thought, and yet nothing has changed. She reached for the single bloom above her and twisted it off its stem. Petal by delicate lavender petal, she crushed the flower between her fingers and dropped it into the street below.

T H I R T E E N

The valley unfurled below her in hues of green and gold. Encircling it was the range of mountains, its ridge tracing the arc of the sun's climb from east to west. Even as Jinda watched, the sun was slipping below the ridge. Soon the domed twilight sky would flatten into darkness.

Standing on the hilltop, she could see Maekung below her, its cluster of thatched roofs tucked among groves of banana trees. Radiating out from the village with the imperfect symmetry of a spiderweb were the brown rice fields.

Had she really been gone? Perhaps time, like water

185

in the deepest section of a river, flowed more slowly here. Perhaps she had never gone to Bangkok at all, never lived there, never worked there, nor witnessed the horror there. Perhaps she had just been out gathering mushrooms all day and was now returning home in the twilight.

She slung her pack over her shoulder and started walking downhill. The path was loosely pebbled, a gentle slope twisting between rock outcrops. She passed the slab of granite where she had often watched butterflies hatching from their cocoons, then the knotted vine dangling from the rain tree where Dao had taught her to swing.

Jinda quickened her steps on the last stretch home. She could imagine her brother drawing water from the well and the look of surprise on his face as she called to him. Then her grandmother would hobble out of the kitchen and peer at her, and her father would run down the steps, tall and strong and laughing, arms outstretched.

Suddenly Jinda's backpack felt unbearably heavy. No, she thought, Father would not be there. He might never run down those steps again.

Jinda walked slowly into the valley. When she reached the village, she found it strangely quiet. A skinny rooster scratched at the dirt, the only sign of life.

She walked through the village. The shutters of most

186

of the houses were closed, and the yards were deserted. It was as if the whole village were in mourning.

And then she was standing in front of her own house. It looked smaller, somehow shrunken. A thick layer of dust coated the wooden boards, and limp morning glory vines draped the fence.

No one was in the yard, but a steady hum of voices, as subdued as the first evening cicadas, drifted out of the house. Jinda felt a sudden wave of uneasiness. What were all those people doing in her house? She slipped past the gate and stood under the mango tree, where she could watch without being seen.

Several lamps were lit, and knots of people, mostly women, huddled on the veranda. Heads bent, their fingers fluttered in the light like nervous moths. They were wrapping, folding, tying things that Jinda could not see.

An old woman glided down the steps and padded over to Nai Wan's yard, where she sliced off a few banana leaves. Back on the veranda, she handed the leaves out to the women.

And only then did Jinda understand.

These women were preparing for a funeral. They had gathered to wrap fermented tea leaves with squares of oiled banana leaf, to fold paper boats and arrange the flowers and candles in each one, to tie little bouquets of pine kindling and incense for the cremation.

But for whose cremation? Her knees suddenly weak,

187

Jinda leaned against a mango tree for support. Immobilized by a sense of dread, she stayed in the shadows as it grew dark.

Soon many of the women rose to leave. A few bustled about, sweeping and picking up things. Finally even the stragglers murmured their good-byes and left.

Jinda's grandmother was left alone. The old woman slipped into the house, but soon she reappeared carrying a stack of clothes in her arms. Her every movement slow and deliberate, she sat down on a mat and set the clothes next to her. She pulled the kerosene lamp to one side and her sewing basket to the other. Carefully, she threaded a needle and picked up the first shirt from the pile. It was Inthorn's.

Hunched over the lamplight, she sewed neat little elbow patches on it, then started to mend the frayed collar. Though a night breeze was blowing, she wore only a thin undershirt, its two straps occasionally slipping down over her shoulders. Her gray hair was tied in a knot at the back of her head, exposing the nape of her delicate neck as she bent over her sewing.

Having mended the shirt, she folded it and reached for another. It looked much like the first one, bleached by years in the sun and countless scrubbings on the stones of the riverbed. This shirt, too, she carefully mended. One by one she went through the little pile, never once pausing or looking up.

The last piece of clothing was Inthorn's jacket. She had made it for him herself, and it had worn well. She held it up in the light now, examining it closely. Only a button from its sleeve was missing. She sewed on a new button, taking great care to align it with its buttonhole. That done, she started folding up the jacket. Then she stopped. Eyes closed, she held the jacket in her arms and rocked it against her gently, to and fro, to and fro. Her thin shoulders shook, but the thick coat muffled the sound of her weeping.

Jinda stood in the shadows and heard, as if from a great distance, a low keening rising from her own throat. She realized now that she had come home too late, and a surge of grief overwhelmed her. Desperately, she crammed handfuls of mango leaves into her mouth to stop up the sobs that welled within her. The crushed leaves tasted of unripe mangoes. Bitter and sharp, she chewed them so that her grief might be silent.

As her sobbing stilled, Jinda took long, shuddering breaths to compose herself. She saw that her grandmother had lifted her face from the jacket and had stopped weeping. Her face twisted into furrows of pain, the woman folded the jacket and laid it over the pile of mended clothes.

Jinda straightened her shoulders and wiped the tears off her cheeks. Only then did she step out from the shadows of the mango tree and call softly to her grandmother.

The funeral for Inthorn Boonrueng took place the next afternoon. Pinit had told Jinda earlier that morn-

189

ing how a prison guard had sent word of their father's worsening health. Unable to get any medical treatment, Inthorn had died shortly after Pinit had written his letter to Sri. She listened to her brother impassively. It did not matter anymore. Her father was shut into a tight wooden coffin now, and details of how he had died seemed unimportant.

In silence she and Pinit had watched as skilled carpenters built a miniature temple of plywood and tinsel for the coffin.

When the miniature temple was finished, the carpenters set it over the coffin, which was then hoisted onto a huge cart laden with flower wreaths and candles. A thick cord was tied to one end of the cart, and it was ready to be pulled to the cremation grounds.

Most of the villagers joined the procession, the men solemn in their starched work shirts and the women severe in their black blouses and black sarongs. Lung Teep, Nai Tong, Sakorn, and several other of Inthorn's close friends took up the rope and, in unison, strained against the weight of the cart. Jinda held the rope with both hands and felt it go taut when the cart began to move.

Pinit and their grandmother were at her side, but Jinda was only vaguely aware of the people around her. The cortege moved slowly on the path to the cremation grounds. To avoid looking at the coffin, Jinda stared at a single piece of tinsel that had worked its

190

way loose from the plywood temple. It fluttered sinuously in the breeze, a strip of silver against the blue sky. Then it caught on a branch and was snapped off. It dangled there, suddenly limp, lifeless. The cremation grounds came into sight, dappled with shade under the canopy of heart-shaped bodhi leaves. Knots of villagers broke off from the procession and hurried toward the shade, dropping down to squat on the gnarled roots of the bodhi trees. Jinda remained in the sun with the coffin until the cart had been dragged into the shady grove.

It was cool and restful under the trees, and a light breeze brushed against her bare arms, drying the prickles of sweat that had formed there. She thought of her father in his narrow coffin, and for a moment she wished he could be brought out to enjoy the breeze.

Three musicians started up. They were swathed in loose black clothes with a white sash around the waist. One played a lute, another a wooden xylophone, which was strapped around his neck, and the third beat a steady rhythm on a long, light drum. The music, at first a mournful metallic wail, grew louder and shriller until the hot air throbbed with it.

The monks started chanting, their sonorous voices competing with the music. Once Jinda would have listened to the stream of incomprehensible Pali words with respect, but today the chanting seemed hollow. The monks were there to help send her father's soul to a better life in his next incarnation. But what had they ever done for him in this life? Had any of them ever worked for his release from his prison cell?

Like polished gourds, the monks' smooth-shaven heads glistened in the sun. One of the novices was scratching his armpit. Another kept swatting at the flies around his ankles.

Their chanting finally over, the monks sprinkled blessed water into the little banana-leaf boats at each corner of the coffin. Then they withdrew, the hems of their orange robes fluttering around them as they walked.

A group of men came forward and took the coffin off the cart. They set it on the ground next to the crematorium and lifted the wooden lid.

It was time for the last farewell.

Jinda's grandmother was the first to go to the open coffin. Her face was impassive. Only her stooped shoulders betrayed any sign of strain. She looked into the coffin for a long moment. Then she laid down her cane, dipped her hands into a bowl of blessed water, and carefully sprinkled it over her dead son.

She called to Pinit to join her and Jinda watched as he, too, stood looking into the coffin. His young face was delicate and open and in his eyes was a bewildered pain. He did not cry, yet there was a darkness about him, as if a passing rain cloud had cast a patch of shadow only on him.

Pinit took a freshly opened coconut and prayed. The

clear, sweet liquid in the coconut was pure, untouched by human hands, and would cleanse Inthorn's soul in preparation for its journey to the next life. Gravely Pinit poured a trickle of the water into the coffin. When he was finished, he looked up at Jinda, his round eyes pleading.

Jinda stepped forward and took the coconut from him. Her hand trembled and a few drops of the liquid splashed out. She walked up to the coffin but could not bear to look into it.

This isn't he, she told herself fiercely. This is not my father anymore. This is just the shell, like an empty cocoon after the moth has flown away. Father has gone. Father is free.

Jinda steeled herself and looked.

And there really was nothing of her father there, nothing but a shell. The hair was grayer, the face more gaunt, the bare feet bony and barely familiar. When she saw his hand, she swallowed hard. She thought of her futile attempt to clean it the day he was arrested and was glad of the chance to wash it one more time. Her hands steady now, she poured the water from the coconut down onto the mangled hand. A few drops of liquid gathered in a little sparkling pool in the palm of the cupped hand.

The lid was put back on the coffin and the coffin placed on the low brick walls of the crematorium. Jinda helped her grandmother back to the shade.

The oldest monk lit the white thread leading to the

193

funeral pyre. The thread burned its way past several branches and finally sparked the oil-soaked kindling beneath the coffin. Within seconds flames leaped up, reaching high into the sky.

The flimsy temple caught fire, its delicate plywood columns sending tendrils of flame up to its tinsel roof and eaves. As Jinda watched, the graceful roof collapsed onto the coffin in a burst of flames, and only a charred skeleton of the pretty temple was left standing, lopsided and crooked.

Trays of funeral bouquets, delicate fans woven of pine kindling and incense, were passed around to the mourners. They each took one and moved as a group toward the pyre. The heat of the flames pressed against Jinda's face and bare arms as she came near the blackened and smoking coffin.

People tossed their pine bouquets into the fire and backed away. Jinda climbed the three steps toward the open fire and looked into it. It was burning so fiercely now that she couldn't even see the coffin anymore. Jinda threw her pine bouquet into the flames and it, too, was swallowed up. She turned away, her eyes stinging.

The ceremony over, most of the mourners drifted out of the grove into the dry heat of the late-afternoon sun. Some broke into light chatter as they walked single file along the bunds of the fields. The monks scattered, too, their bright orange robes looking like sparks of ember blown from the funeral fire across the bleached countryside.

Only some of Inthorn's friends remained, squatting in a small circle. They didn't play games of dice to pass the time or laugh and talk with gruff tenderness about the deceased, as was the usual custom. This was not the ordinary funeral of a man who had lived out his life fully and died peacefully.

Jinda leaned against a big bodhi tree and pressed her cheeks onto its rough bark. What had it all been for? A few more bushels of rice? Surely her father's life had been worth more than that. Ned would say that Inthorn had given his life for a cause, an idea—justice, equality, democracy. It seemed so remote now.

Jinda stared at the funeral fire. A few flakes of ash, skimmed up by a passing breeze, scattered into the air. One flake blew past her, and she reached out and caught it. When she opened her hand, there was only a faint smudge of gray on her palm. From flesh to ash, from blood to smoke—had her father died just for some vague, unrealized dream?

Jinda did not return to the bodhi grove where her father's ashes lay, even when her family went to collect his bones the day after the cremation. She hated the bodhi grove with its gloomy shadows and smell of ashes and death. She hated the thought of her father reduced to the crumbs of charred bone that were now enshrined in a little urn on the family altar. Jinda did not want to brood over her father's death. He was gone, and no amount of mourning would bring him back. She was the head of the household now, and she decided it was up to her to plan for the family's future.

In the two months that she had been away in Bangkok, the house had fallen into even worse disrepair. Many of the planks on the veranda had warped or rotted. The roof needed rethatching, and the bamboo fencing sagged under the weight of untrimmed vines. Refusing any offers of help from her neighbors, Jinda started the repairs of the house alone, with fierce energy.

Sometimes, caught up in work, she looked up and glared accusingly at anyone she thought was not working hard enough. Once, when she was repairing a section of fence by the well, she saw Pinit sitting nearby, his chin cupped in his hands.

"What are you doing?" she demanded.

"Nothing."

"Well, why don't you do something?"

"Like what?" Pinit asked timidly.

Jinda hacked at the morning glory vines draped over the fence with such savagery that she split part of the bamboo railing. "I don't care!" she cried. "Just don't sit there!" Then, flinging down her sickle, Jinda stalked off.

"Why is she always angry?" she heard Pinit ask their grandmother as she fled the yard.

"She is not angry, child," the old woman said. "She is just determined not to be sad."

The fierce, restless anger that Jinda nurtured did help to keep the sadness at bay. But sometimes, when she felt too exhausted to stoke her anger anymore, she retreated to a quiet spot on a nearby hilltop and allowed the sadness to permeate her.

Her retreat was a spot where she and Dao had passed many happy hours in their childhood, watching butterflies hatch from their cocoons, swinging from the knotted vine dangling from the rain tree, or just sitting quietly chatting the long afternoon away.

Now that Dao was no longer home, the spot seemed forlorn and neglected. Whenever Jinda sat here, her thoughts often turned to Dao. She wondered if her sister had deliberately forgotten about her. Ever since Dao had moved out of Maekung, she had not returned home once, nor had she sent any message back to her family.

At first Jinda had worried about her sister, but the worry had gradually turned to a sharp bitterness. Jinda imagined Dao living a life of luxury in town with her Mr. Dusit. Fine, don't come back, Jinda told her sister silently. We don't need you, either.

Jinda also brooded about Ned. She worried that he

might have been hurt the day of the massacre, that he might have been arrested or be in hiding somewhere. Since leaving Bangkok she had had no word from him, and the silence had frustrated and frightened her.

She had written to Sri at her Prathipat address, asking for news. But Sri had replied in a note so cautious that Jinda knew better than to write her again. Sri was working at a private hospital, her note simply said, and did not keep in touch with any of her old friends anymore.

With no news from her sister or her friends, Jinda felt isolated and cut off from the outside world. She would sit, hugging her knees to her, staring across the valley at the path connecting Maekung to the world beyond.

Sometimes, as she gazed at the narrow, twisting path, she would imagine Ned climbing down that trail again. But evening after evening would fade into darkness, and still there would be no sign of Ned. Tired and dispirited, Jinda would walk back alone to the village.

Yet, the next day, she would be back at that spot, gazing at the winding path.

One afternoon in February, Jinda climbed to this spot and stared at the landscape. The stretch of bone-dry fields was relieved only by clumps of tasseled weeds whose feathery plumes swayed in the breeze. Here and there, a charred tree stump dotted the hillside. The dusty road that linked Maekung to the nearest town wound up the other side of the valley.

Jinda leaned against a teak sapling, watching a black beetle attack a dragonfly with a torn wing. Idly she picked up a pebble and crushed the beetle. But saving the maimed dragonfly gave her no satisfaction. As it crawled away, twitching its wings weakly, Jinda reached out and crushed the dragonfly too. Then she tossed the pebble away and watched it roll down the hill.

Suddenly Jinda sat up straight.

In the distance, a tiny figure climbed the hillside. Ned? Jinda thought with a surge of hope, her heart pounding.

She squinted against the afternoon sun. The figure moved slowly, pausing in the shade of a tree. There it lifted both arms to fumble at the back of its head. A cascade of thick black hair slipped down, then was gathered and reknotted again with a deft twist. It was a gesture Jinda had seen hundreds of times.

Dao, she realized, with a stab of disappointment.

Dao resumed climbing, and when she approached Jinda's spot, Jinda could see that her clothes were soaked through with sweat and her breathing ragged.

"Welcome home," Jinda said loudly. Her voice was harsh and tense and held no real welcome in it.

Startled, Dao looked up. "Jinda!" she said, her face crinkling into a smile. Then she saw her sister's disapproving frown, and her smile faded. "You didn't expect to see me, did you?" she asked.

Jinda stared at her impassively. "I did at Father's

funeral," she said. "But when you didn't return even for that—well, I never expected you again," she said.

Dao dropped her eyes and sighed. "I wanted very much to be here for Father's funeral," she said in a low voice. She dragged herself up the last few feet toward Jinda, then sank down on a log under the same tree.

For a moment neither of them spoke. Dao stole a look at her sister. "I would have come back for the funeral, Jinda, but my . . . my relationship with Dusit was really shaky then, and I wanted so much to . . . to make it strong again. I thought that if only I had his child, he would . . ."

Jinda glanced up sharply at her sister. Her hair was streaked brown with dust, and her blouse was shabby and wrinkled. She looked unkempt and tired. But what caught Jinda's attention was the distinct bulge under her sister's sarong. "You're pregnant," Jinda said.

Dao nodded miserably. "I thought Dusit and I would become a real couple if we had a child together," she said.

"And . . . ?"

"Dusit has someone else now—someone younger and slimmer than I." Dao wiped her sweat-glazed face on a frayed sleeve, and her hand fell listlessly on her lap. There was, Jinda noted, no longer a red-jeweled ring flashing on it.

In a tired voice, Dao talked about the last eight months since she had left Maekung. Dusit had treated

200

her royally at first, she said, buying her new clothes and renting her an apartment with fancy furniture and even running water. He had also assured her that he would secure special permission for her to visit her father regularly.

"But I never saw him," Dao whispered, avoiding Jinda's eyes. "I don't think Dusit ever really meant for me to visit him. It was just one of the many false promises he made to get me to live with him." She had kicked off her rubber sandals now, and for a while she remained silent, tracing circles in the sand with her toe.

"You should never have listened to him," Jinda said.

Dao laughed, but it was a weak and brittle sound. "That's easy for you to say now," she said.

"I said it before too, Dao. What do you expect from a man like Dusit?"

"Nothing," Dao said, hunched over her bulging abdomen like a maimed insect. "But, oh, Jinda, have pity! If not for me, at least for this little unborn one. The baby has done you no wrong. I want him to grow up with you, with our family around to care for him. I want Granny to rock him to sleep, and Pinit to play with him." She stopped and smiled at Jinda uncertainly. "And I want you to bathe him. Just the way we used to bathe little Oi in the river, remember?"

Jinda looked at the range of mountains encircling their valley and at the shadows they made across the rice fields. In the distance she could hear Pinit's cowbell as he brought the buffalo home. She remembered the afternoon she and Dao had sat here after Oi was cremated.

"I remember," Jinda answered quietly. She reached out and put her hand against her sister's cheek. "Welcome home, Dao," she said. And this time she meant it.

F O U R T E E N

Dao slipped back into village life so quietly it was as if she had never left. Her grandmother, refraining from asking her any questions, had simply welcomed her back with open arms. And if some of the village women gossiped about Dao behind her back, a few caustic words from her grandmother quickly silenced them. Within a week, Dao was back with her old group of friends, drying chili peppers in the sun or mending clothes as she chatted the afternoon away.

And so February passed into the hot, dry days of March and April. The gay water-splashing of the Songkran Festival brought a few days of relief, but then the heat and the quiet monotony of the dry season took over again. Jinda did not mind the hot weather, especially since there was little work that needed to be done in the fields before the rains came, but Dao, her belly steadily swelling, found the relentless heat a burden.

When May passed without any hint of rain, Jinda began to worry. Another drought as bad as the one the year before, she knew, would mean real suffering for the villagers.

By June, there was still no sign of the monsoon rains. Like the other villagers, Jinda and Dao decided to go ahead and start the seedbed anyway. If it did rain, at least the seedlings would be ready to transplant.

Jinda plowed and harrowed a tiny plot in the fields, carefully digging a narrow irrigation ditch around the raised seedbed.

In the meantime Dao soaked two buckets of un-husked rice grain in a shallow basket of water. She skimmed off the empty grains that floated to the top, poured the remaining grains into a basket lined with damp straw, and left it to germinate.

The rice seed had sprouted tiny green shoots within a few days. The two sisters dragged the basket to the fields and broadcast the seedlings onto the seedbed. For days, they watched over the seedbed anxiously, waiting for the grain to take root and send up new shoots through the mud.

That had been weeks ago, and still there had been very little rain. The seedbed was drying up and the tender seedlings shriveling. Day after day, Jinda, Dao and Pinit had carried buckets of water from the river to the seedbed and managed to keep the seedlings alive.

And now the hardest part was before them. Plowing the dry fields beyond the seedbed was traditionally a

204

man's work, but Pinit was too young to do the work his father had always done. Jinda was forced to try it on her own.

Jinda yoked the heavy wooden plow onto their water buffalo and tried her best to plow the eight *rai* of land Inthorn had farmed. The soil was dry and unyielding, and she had to push down onto the plowshare with all her strength just to break through the hard crust. She wished fervently that the monsoon rains would come soon, so that the damp earth would soften enough to make plowing easier. As it was, there had been a few scattered showers, and then long dry spells.

Jinda wiped the sweat streaming from her face and leaned against the plow. She had been plowing all morning, yet she had barely finished half a small field. The furrow in front of her was shallow and crooked, not at all like the deep, straight lines her father had carved into the soil with such seeming ease. Even the buffalo had been uncooperative, ignoring her desperate cries of "Right! To the right!" to lumber clumsily over bunds into adjoining fields.

Soaked with sweat and breathing hard, Jinda scanned the sky. In the distance, clumps of gray clouds were massing behind the mountain ridge, but not nearly enough for the long, heavy downpour they would need before the fields could be plowed a second time.

Dao, her big belly jutting out before her, waddled across the field to Jinda, carefully avoiding the clods of soil in the new furrow.

"Still no sign of rain?" Dao sighed.

Jinda shook her head gloomily.

"Here, let me help plow a little at least," Dao said.

Gently Jinda pried her sister's hand off the wooden plow handle. "Don't be silly," she said. "You're too close to your time to do this."

"But you look so tired," Dao said. "You need help. Admit it. We could ask some friends to help us."

"Like who?" Jinda asked wearily. "Nai Tong and Lung Teep?" They both knew that their father's closest friends had disappeared from the village shortly after his funeral, most probably to join the Communist forces in the mountains nearby. Their wives claimed, quite unconvincingly, that they had gone to find work in the city.

"Actually," Dao said, "I was thinking of someone younger and . . . " she hesitated.

"Unmarried?" Jinda finished for her. "Why don't you just say it, Dao? Just tell me to get married to Vichai, or Somboon, or Surin, so we'll have some help with the plowing. That's what you want, isn't it?"

"What's so wrong with that?" Dao asked.

When Jinda remained silent, Dao gently shook her by the shoulders. "You're still waiting for Ned, aren't you?" Dao demanded. "Listen, sister, he won't come back. Men never do. I waited for Ghan, but he never came back, not even when he knew I was carrying his child. And I've waited for Dusit, yes, even now, hoping he might come for this child's birth. But he won't come. I know he won't. I admit it. You should too, Jinda. Accept the fact that Ned is never going to come back here."

Jinda turned away. At the edge of the valley the mountains loomed stark and brown. She had gazed at them countless times, watching for some sign of Ned, hoping to see him climbing down the trail again.

It had been eight months now since Jinda had caught her last glimpse of Ned, standing on the platform above the crowd as the bombs exploded, his arm raised as if in farewell to her. Eight months—and not a word from him. He could be in prison, or in exile, or even dead. But then again, he might be free—in hiding, or with the Communist guerrillas in the jungle like Nai Tong. And if he was free, Jinda told herself, if he was free, he would come for her. She had to keep believing that. It was all she had left to believe in.

"I don't need any help," Jinda said at last. "I can manage alone." Taking a deep breath, she urged the buffalo to move.

"Don't be so stubborn!" Dao shouted, reaching out to restrain Jinda. Just then the plow lurched forward and knocked Dao off her feet. Dao screamed and fell heavily on a row of rice stubble.

Jinda sprang forward to help her sister. Dao's face was twisted with pain, and she clutched at her stomach, moaning softly. She looked dazed.

207

Jinda tried to help Dao to her feet, and she noticed a stain soaking into the dry dust on Dao's sarong. "You are bleeding," she said, frightened.

Dao stared at the wet spot. "It isn't blood," she said slowly. "My water must have broken."

"Does that mean the baby might . . . the baby might—" Jinda stopped. She had no idea what the baby might do.

"The baby might come early," Dao said. "I had better get home to Granny right now." Awkwardly, she tried to get up but was too clumsy to manage.

Jinda half lifted, half pulled Dao upright. Her face was beaded with sweat, and strands of wet hair struck to her cheeks. Without a word, the two sisters started home, leaving the buffalo to gaze impassively after them.

Late that afternoon, after Jinda had helped her grandmother settle Dao comfortably in the bedroom, she came back out to the fields to finish plowing. As she neared the edge of the fields, she saw a shadow move in the bamboo grove.

There was a rustling sound, and then she thought she heard someone whisper her name. She looked around. It was twilight, and a breeze was blowing, so that everywhere shadows were moving and leaves rustling. Jinda wondered if she had only imagined the whisper.

Leaving the plow, she walked closer to the bamboo grove.

"Jinda! Over here!"

This time there was no mistaking it. Someone hidden behind the bamboo leaves was calling softly to her. Her heart beating fast, Jinda stepped into the shadows of the bamboo grove and saw a man crouched there.

It was Ned.

His face was gaunt, his clothes were torn, and in his eyes was a hunted look. He wore a dark-blue farmer's workshirt, which flapped open, revealing an amulet of a small Buddha hung from a string. He had grown so thin that his shoulder blades jutted out sharply.

He glanced furtively behind Jinda. "Nobody saw me?" he asked.

Jinda shook her head. She did not trust herself to speak.

"I've been here all afternoon," he whispered hoarsely, "waiting for you to come close enough."

Gone was his easy confidence. He sounded strained, as if he were used to whispering and was now making a special effort to speak up. The alertness in him that had once reminded Jinda of a stalking tiger now seemed only like the nervousness of a nocturnal animal on the prowl. From the hunter to the hunted, Jinda thought with a flash of pain.

"It has been a long time," she said shakily. "Where have you been?"

"In hiding, mostly," Ned said, and he tried to smile.

It was such a brave yet pathetic effort that impulsively Jinda reached out and took his hand in hers. Large and bony, with round, smooth knuckles, it seemed reassuringly familiar. But the once-smooth palms were rough and callused now, the fingernails rimmed with dirt. The thought that Ned had a farmer's hand at last made her smile. "I am glad you're safe," she said.

"And I am glad you are," he answered simply.

For a moment neither of them spoke. Cocooned by the rustling leaves, Jinda allowed herself to feel a wave of relief and happiness.

"I hoped you would come, but I was not sure," Jinda said. "I thought you might have been arrested, or hurt. I saw so many others hurt. That little shoeshine boy, I saw his hands. . . ." An image of delicate wrists, dripping from the tamarind tree, flashed across her mind, and she swallowed hard.

"Don't think about it anymore," Ned said.

"I have to know. Did it get much worse? After I left? Did you see . . ." She wanted to ask him about the horrors recorded in black and white on that roll of film Sri had brought in. But she could find no words to describe them.

"I saw things that I will not forget," Ned said. "And that I don't want to talk about."

"Some nights I wake up crying," Jinda persisted.

"The dreams are so bad. I still hear the screams, the gunfire. And the smell from that awful fire."

Ned put his hand on Jinda's arm and held it firmly. "It's over," he said. "Reliving it won't bring the dead back to life. We have survived it. And we have to start all over again."

"Start all over again," Jinda echoed softly. Hadn't Ned used the same words around the campfire the first night he had arrived at Maekung? The words had sounded so noble and mysterious then, and she had been intrigued by them. But hearing them now, Jinda sensed that Ned meant something different this time. Together they would start over again, and that togetherness would make all the difference in the world. Jinda could feel her heart lifting. Together they would work to build a home. Together they would plow the fields, transplant the rice seedlings, harvest the next crop. Together they would build a new life!

She felt a rush of tenderness for him, for how frail and bony he had become. "Let me get you something to eat," she said.

He looked at her gratefully. "I have not eaten since yesterday," he answered.

Hurriedly, Jinda led the buffalo home and tethered him under the rice barn. Wanting to avoid her family, Jinda climbed the stairs as quietly as possible.

But her caution was unnecessary. No one noticed her, and she was able to take half a pot of leftover rice and some salted vegetables from the kitchen without anyone asking her about it.

It was only as she was leaving the house that she heard Dao groaning in the bedroom. For a moment, Jinda considered going back upstairs to Dao, but then she heard her grandmother's soothing voice and decided that Ned needed the food more urgently than Dao needed her. I will be back soon to help you, she promised Dao silently as she slipped off.

By the time she returned to the bamboo grove, the sun had set, and it was dark. Ned was curled up in a corner asleep, his head nestled in his arms. He looked young and vulnerable, his long eyelashes casting feathery shadows against his cheeks. Jinda sat down beside him and just gazed at him, her heart filled with joy.

Finally she nudged him awake and offered him a dipper of water.

Ned stretched and gave her a slow, sleepy smile. Reaching for the dipper with both hands, he drank in graceless gulps, the water trickling out the corners of his mouth and staining his dust-streaked neck. When he had drained it, he looked up and thanked Jinda.

The space behind the bamboo leaves was cool and shady, and Jinda sat on a patch of mossy ground. Ned faced her, an arm's length away. Wordlessly, Jinda handed him the food, and as wordlessly Ned started to eat it. Jinda watched him eat, and her heart ached.

Here is the man who told us we need never be hungry, she thought, who told us dreams were worth fighting for and dying for. He urged us to fight for more—more land, more food, more "rights." And in the end what have we gained? Just another man who is as hungry as the rest of us.

And yet, watching him finish every last grain of rice, Jinda felt no bitterness, or contempt, or even pity. Instead, she was grateful that he had really become one of them now, so that it would be natural for him to settle down and make his home in Maekung.

"What are you thinking about?" Ned asked her quietly.

Jinda flushed. "Nothing much," she said. "About what you said earlier, about starting over again."

Ned smiled. "That's what I was thinking about too," he said.

The words flowed from both of them easily after that. Jinda told him of her father's death and the funeral, and of Dao's returning home pregnant. "In fact, she is due at any moment now," Jinda added, remembering the low moans she had heard earlier that evening. "I should go back soon and see how she is doing." But Jinda made no move to leave yet.

Instead she listened to Ned as he talked of his life as a fugitive. He described how he had wrested himself free of the police at the rally, as his supporters had sprung to his rescue, and escaped into the crowd. For months he had lived in hiding, he said, slipping "like a shadow" from one friend's house to another,

213

trying to reorganize the remnants of the student network. Failing that, in desperation he had made contact with the Communist guerrillas whose base camps were in remote mountains.

"I am sorry I didn't get in touch with you, Jinda," he said, "but I did think of you a lot, and I wanted to be with you again. Very much."

The moon had risen without either of them noticing, its pale light filtering down from the canopy of bamboo leaves. Ned stopped talking and leaned over to touch Jinda's cheek with his fingertips. She sat very still as Ned stroked her face, her neck, then her bare arms.

"Touch me," Ned whispered, so softly that it sounded like the rustle of leaves overhead. "Touch me, Jinda," he said again.

He took off his shirt, and his bare chest gleamed in the moonlight. Cautiously, Jinda reached out and touched him.

His chest was cool and hard, like the slabs of stone on the riverbed polished smooth by years of running water. She touched him with both hands, her fingers fanning out along the delicate ridge of his collarbone and over his chest.

"So hard," Jinda whispered. How lean and strong a man's body was. Hard where a woman was soft, like the plow blade against the soft, moist earth.

"When the rains come, you can plow our land," Jinda said. She let Ned hold her wrists and lift her palms toward his mouth. He kissed each hand, and she felt a strange, tingling sensation. "And a spice garden," she said dreamily. "And a new thatched roof, and children too."

Ned held her hands away from him a little and looked at her. "What are you talking about, Jinda?" he asked.

"About the life we are going to share," Jinda answered. "About starting over again, the way you said. Ned, why are you looking at me like that? Don't you want children? And a home with a spice garden . . ."

Ned let go of her hands and took a deep breath. For a moment he said nothing. Then he shook his head and said gently, "Our life together isn't going to be about babies and spice gardens, Jinda. At least mine isn't."

Jinda could hardly form her words. "What do you mean?" she asked shakily.

"Don't you understand? I have joined the Thai Communists. I am on my way to their northern base camp right now."

"What about me?" Jinda asked, her voice choked.

"I want you to come back with me. To the jungle, Jinda, to join me in the struggle for justice and equa—"

"No!" The word leaped out of her mouth before she could check it.

"But why not? You said you wanted to build a life with me—"

"Yes, but . . . but, I meant together—at home!"

"In Maekung?"

"Yes, in Maekung," Jinda said, sitting up straight now and talking very earnestly. "We can plow the fields together and plant this year's rice. The rains will come, I know they will. And after the harvest, we could—"

"We could hand over half of our crop to Dusit?"

"We'll still have the other half," Jinda said imploringly. "Maybe someday it'll change, but—"

"Someday! Someday will never come unless we fight for it, Jinda. Haven't the last few months taught you anything? We have to fight for what we want."

Jinda's heart sank. "Fight? You mean with guns?"

"It has come to that," Ned said.

"You would shoot a gun, wound people, kill them?" Jinda's voice shook. "The way they did to us at the rally?"

"Believe me, Jinda, I don't want to," Ned said. "But I have tried peaceful means. Liberal dissent, parliamentary reform—all the things that are supposed to work in a democracy. Where did they get us? The military took over without our even putting up a struggle. Just like that, they are back in control of the government. Don't you see, Jinda? The only thing the military understands is force. They shot at us; we have got to shoot back at them. It is that simple."

Jinda shook her head. "Killing people," she said miserably, "is never that simple."

216

"You would never have to shoulder a gun, Jinda," Ned said quickly. "Especially since Sri's already taught you some basic first aid. You could help nurse the wounded. There are always wounded guerrillas after every skirmish with the government soldiers."

"I have had enough of fighting!" Jinda protested.

"But don't you see? There is no other way," Ned said. "Violence is the only way to overthrow the ruling class and achieve justice and equality—"

"Justice!" Jinda said fiercely. "Can you taste justice? Can you smell equality? What do all your fancy words mean? I can't live my life for things that I can't taste, or smell, or hold in my hands. Soil after the rain, it has such a rich, sweet smell. And tamarind shoots leave a golden taste on your tongue. These things are real. These things I can live for."

"But Jinda—"

"No, let me finish. I don't want to see any more bloodshed. My father died before his time for these empty words. I—"

"Your father died," Ned broke in angrily, "fighting for a better life for us all. I have got to fight on so that he didn't die in vain. Can't you understand that? Doesn't his death mean anything to you?"

"Yes, it does!" Jinda replied, trying to keep her voice steady. "It means that he is gone forever. It means I don't want you to die all for some vague dream, either! I want you to live with me, to work the soil that my father worked before, and yes, to raise some fat babies. I want to live, and grow things, and be happy. Is that so wrong?"

Jinda was not prepared for the tears that rolled down Ned's cheeks, leaving shiny streaks that reflected the moonlight. "No, that is not wrong," he said, very softly. "I want that too, very much," and his voice was so filled with longing that Jinda felt her eyes sting. "But I am not ready for that, Jinda. There is too much I must do first." He turned away, hugging his knees to him.

He looked thin and fragile, and yet, Jinda realized with a slow wonder, he had a kind of strength nothing would snap.

Slowly, Jinda lay down on the moss. The crescent moon shone through the lacy mesh of bamboo leaves above her. Only the whir of the cicadas broke the utter stillness of the night. Jinda felt a great weight of sadness and fatigue descend on her.

Ned uncurled his long arms and legs and stretched out next to her. He reached over and drew her to him. Intuitively, so naturally that it seemed she had slept this way every night of her life, she put her head on his shoulder and snuggled against him. Through her thin blouse she could feel his warmth, and she pressed herself against that. Drowsily she marveled at how wonderful it was to fall asleep in a bamboo grove.

* * *

Jinda awoke with a start. Had she imagined it, or was that thunder rumbling in the distance? A bolt of lightning flashed in the west, followed by another roll of thunder. Jinda's pulse quickened. Suppose the monsoon rains suddenly came. How would they manage to do everything in time? There was the plowing to be finished, then the harrowing, and mending of dikes, and the transplanting. If only Ned would come back with her and help.

Jinda looked down at Ned wistfully. He was still asleep, his arms flung up over his head, his chest rising and falling evenly. He looked very young. She touched his cheek gently. He stirred, blinked, and looked up at her.

"Is it morning?" he asked drowsily.

Jinda nodded.

"So soon," he said.

"So soon," Jinda repeated sadly.

They did not say anything again for some time. The dawn light sifted through the leaves, dappling a starling perched on a branch above them. When Ned stood up, it flew away, soundlessly.

"Won't . . . won't you change your mind?" Jinda asked.

"Won't you?" he answered.

Jinda shook her head, and Ned shook his. They exchanged a brief, sad smile. Then he picked up the

219

backpack he had with him and slung it over his shoulder.

"If . . . if you ever want to come back," Jinda said, "you know I will be here."

He gazed at her for a long time. Then he said gravely, "I know that, Jinda."

He turned and walked away without looking back.

She watched him make his way up a steep, craggy path on the mountainside. Lithe and surefooted, he climbed with the confident stride of a tiger, a fighter again. Sad though she was at seeing him leave, she felt a surge of pride in him.

Ned reached the top of the hill and turned around. Silhouetted against the morning sky, he lifted one arm in an expansive farewell. Jinda tried to smile, but she knew he was already too far away to see it.

Once Ned disappeared over the crest of that hill, Jinda's first impulse was to run after him and offer to go with him after all. She started to run, then stopped abruptly. He didn't need her. He would welcome her, of course, but he didn't really need her. Not the way Dao did. Not the way Pinit and her grandmother did. Not the way the land, that dry, barren land did.

Dark storm clouds were gathering on the horizon, and a brisk wind seemed to be blowing them toward the valley. Silently Jinda prayed for the rains to start.

Slowly she walked back toward the village. Near her house she saw Pinit shooting clay marbles with a group of children. She paused to say hello to him, but her sentence was cut short by a loud, shrill scream.

"Dao!" Jinda cried, recognizing her sister's voice. She turned and ran home. When she had climbed the ladder and reached the doorway of the inner room, she stopped.

Dao had crawled off the sleeping mat. On her hands and knees, she was groaning loudly, her whole body rigid. Her hair had fallen over her face, and her clothes were in disarray. She swayed to and fro, her back arched. Then her moans subsided, and she sank back onto the floor.

Jinda tiptoed into the room and approached her sister. "Dao," she murmured.

Her sister's eyelids fluttered open. "Where were you?" she whispered.

Jinda smoothed back some strands of Dao's hair. "With Ned," she said.

A look of disbelief crossed Dao's face. "Ned? He's . . . here?"

"He's gone," Jinda said, managing a crooked little grin. "And I'm still here. So don't worry about it."

"But you and Ned . . ."

"We decided to go separate ways. He wants to fight, and I . . ."—she paused—"I want to grow things." She could feel a sharp sting in her eyes, and hastily she blinked her tears away.

Their grandmother, sitting by the window, took a deep puff from her cigar and blew some smoke at Jinda thoughtfully. "We are glad you came back, child," she said. "Who knows? Maybe someday he will come back too."

The old woman finished her cigar, then stubbed it out on the windowsill. She turned to Jinda and became businesslike.

"Now that you are back, I will need you to help me. The baby is due any moment. Go cut me a stack of fresh banana leaves," she told Jinda briskly. "And get me that big kettle of boiled water. One more thing, cut me a sliver of bamboo, about the length of a knife blade. Notch the bamboo, and then pry it open with your hands. Split the bamboo down the middle, but be sure not to touch the sharp edge inside. It must be kept absolutely clean. Understand?"

Glad to have something to do, Jinda left the room. Outside, the wind had increased, and the broad, flat banana leaves flapped wildly about the spongy trunks as Jinda slashed off leaves one by one. When she had about six leaves tucked under her arm, she brought them back to the house and put them on the veranda.

Then she set off to the bamboo grove and chose a clean, brittle pole growing on the edge of the grove. The pole was tough, but after a brief struggle Jinda chopped through it. She made a notch along it, then ripped it down the middle. The edge that was exposed was sharp and clean. Untouched by human hand, this sliver of bamboo would be used to cut the baby's umbilical cord.

The wind was so fierce now that it whipped the sharp bamboo leaves in her face, stinging her cheeks. Head bent, Jinda pushed her way out of the grove and stumbled back to the house. Heavy clouds of dust and sand swirled about her ankles. Wooden shutters were slammed shut on the neighboring houses.

Would the wind blow the rain clouds right past them? Squinting against the dust, Jinda scanned the sky. But another shrill cry came from the house, and Jinda hurried inside.

Dao was in the middle of another contraction. Gripping the pillows on either side of the mat, her arms anchored her writhing body onto the floor. The veins in her neck bulged as she moaned. Then the spasm of pain passed, and Dao went limp.

Through the rest of the morning, Jinda cradled her sister's head in her lap, brushing the hair back from her eyes, feeding her sips of cool well water, and massaging her back after each spasm.

Once a gust of wind blew a clump of leaves through the window, flinging them in a swirling eddy against the walls. Dao grabbed one and crushed it into tiny fragments.

In the late afternoon, as a painful contraction passed, her grandmother knelt down and massaged Dao's legs. "It's almost over, child," she said. "Rest when you can. There, close your eyes." She talked soothingly until Dao's breathing became more regular.

The pain began again. Jinda saw Dao tense herself for another contraction, but it never came. Instead, Dao struggled to sit up. The old woman pushed her back down gently.

Dao grunted, straining. "I have to . . ."

"You want to push? Go ahead. Push, woman!" her grandmother said.

Grimacing, Dao grabbed onto her sister's hands and pushed. Her breathing came in sharp, erratic pants, and she squeezed her eyes shut as she strained.

Deftly the old woman undid the knot of Dao's sarong and draped the cloth up over Dao's knees. Then she ducked down, her face disappearing between Dao's spread legs. When she reemerged over the edge of the sarong, she was smiling.

"It is coming," she said. "I can see a bit of its head. You are almost there, Dao. Hold on tight, there, and push again!" The old woman calmly spread out the stack of powder-smooth banana leaves under Dao's buttocks and legs so that there was a double lining of leaves over the mat.

Dao hung onto Jinda's hands. Low, long grunts seemed to well up from deep within her as she squeezed the baby downward.

"I can't . . . oh, I can't . . . , " she gasped.

Abruptly she let go of Jinda's hands and pressed down hard against her own belly, as if trying to block the outward surge. "Stop it," Dao cried, ". . . too big!"

But her grandmother pried Dao's hands away and placed her own hands on the heaving womb. Instinctively, she sensed when every new muscle contraction would crest, and she squeezed Dao's abdomen slowly and gently, pressing on the mound.

"Jinda," she murmured, "spread her legs wider. Go on, child, this is no time to be shy! And lift her sarong up more. Can you see the baby's head?"

225

Hesitantly, Jinda looked. Between the vertical folds of her sister's opening, she saw what seemed to be a patch of slick black hair. Each time Dao pushed, the folds of flesh were pulled wider apart, like reluctant curtains being drawn, and a fraction more of the slick patch was revealed.

"I can see it," Jinda said breathlessly.

Rammed against Dao's torn opening, the head looked huge, and still it continued to expand. Rounder, fuller, it pressed outward. And then suddenly the baby was coming out, its domed head completely through, its slender neck sprouting between Dao's legs like a stalk. Before Jinda could reach for it, the rest slithered out—chest, arms, and legs. Slim and slippery and blue-gray, it looked like a catfish squirming out of a mud puddle.

Jinda touched it. It was warm and wet. Moist hair plastered against its forehead, eyes shut, its tiny fists clenched. Jinda noted with some satisfaction that it was a fighter. Awkwardly, she held it up toward Dao, her hand cupping its smooth, moist buttocks.

"A girl," Jinda heard her grandmother say to Dao.

She looked down at the creature in her hands. Yes, she was already a tiny replica of her mother, complete with a tiny set of petallike folds like the ones from which she had just emerged. Jinda was glad it was a girl.

Her grandmother was kneading Dao's stomach with a firm, vigorous rhythm. Dao groaned and flung out her arm to brush the old woman's hands off, but it was a feeble gesture.

As her grandmother continued to press, the afterbirth was delivered. With a rush of blood, the slick, dark placenta slipped out, forming a puddle on the banana leaves. Jinda noticed that her own hands were smeared with blood.

For a split second, images of the student massacre flashed through Jinda's mind. Blood-streaked bodies piled into ambulances, severed wrists dripping blood from the tamarind tree, and now her own blood-stained hands. Jinda fought down a wave of nausea.

The old woman was tying a knot around the pulsating umbilical cord, inches away from the baby. Her gnarled hands were trembling badly.

"Help me cut this," Jinda's grandmother said, handing the bamboo sliver to Jinda. She pointed to the knot on the umbilical cord.

Jinda felt the piece of sharp bamboo being thrust into her hand. She felt dizzy with the sight and smell of blood. "I . . . I can't . . . , " she said hoarsely.

And then the baby cried. It was a triumphant sound, strong and sweet with the pulse of life. There is the blood of death and the blood of life, Jinda suddenly realized. And this blood on her hands was the blood of life. Jinda took a deep breath and felt better. Her hand held the bamboo blade without a tremor now. Quickly she bent down and slashed through the cord, still turgid with the flow of Dao's blood to her child. The cut was clean and sharp.

The baby wailed.

"Listen to her!" Jinda called to her sister.

Dao was listening, but not to the baby. Startled, her eyes wide with wonder, she was staring out the open window.

Only then did Jinda hear it too: a quick, frantic hammering all around them. The roof, the walls, the leaves outside were trembling with the sound. The whole room pulsed with it. Unbelieving, holding her breath, Jinda looked out the window.

It was raining.

"She has brought the rain," Dao said, holding out her arms for the baby.

Jinda held the slippery little creature toward her sister. The baby whimpered, waving one tiny fist in the air.

"Wash her," Dao said softly.

"We will, child," her grandmother said. "You lie back down. Rest."

"No. Wash her," Dao insisted. "Now. In the rain."

And so Jinda took the baby in her arms, a damp, limp thing, and walked outside. Fresh gusts of wind blew under the eaves, tearing bits of thatching with it. Jinda stepped out from the shelter of the eaves and onto the open veranda, holding the baby close to her.

Daughter of the rain, she said silently, here—meet the sky. The rain was warm and gentle, coursing down

Jinda's face and onto the tiny baby. She watched the raindrops stream over its smooth skin, rinsing away the smears of blood.

Jinda sat down at the top of the steps, holding the baby in her lap. A pool of rainwater slowly collected in her sarong. With one hand she held the baby's limp neck and with the other she scooped the rainwater from her lap to bathe the baby.

Other villagers were tumbling out of their houses, laughing up at the sky. Children tore off mud-caked clothes and ran naked in the warm rain, their bare buttocks slick and brown. Housewives moved woven baskets of herb gardens out into the rain, while men pushed glazed urns under bamboo drains to catch the rain from the roofs. And in one corner of the yard, an old man stood alone, his face uplifted to catch the raindrops on his tongue.

Jinda watched them happily as the water in her lap became tinted a pale red from bloodstains. The rain pelted down harder, stinging her scalp and cheeks. The baby started to cry.

"Give her to me!" Jinda's grandmother called from the doorway.

Getting up, Jinda handed the baby, now glistening clean, back to her grandmother.

"Is Dao all right?" Jinda asked, as together they wrapped the baby tightly in the old checkered shawl Oi had used last year.

"She's resting," her grandmother said.

"So you don't need any more help?"

The old woman smiled, shaking her head. "Go ahead," she said. "Go run in the rain. If I could run, I would be outside running too!"

Jinda flashed her a smile, then ran down the steps of the veranda and out the swinging bamboo gate. The earth was soft and pliant under her bare feet. How good to feel mud again!

Out in the lane, the wind grew stronger. A gust slashed against Jinda's arms, stinging them as if with long, sharp rice stalks. She passed the hibiscus hedge and saw its leaves streaked a bright green where the rain had washed off the thick layers of dust. A few flowers burst through, cleansed a brilliant scarlet by the rain.

Sprinting down the lane, Jinda's steps were light and springy against the mud-slick soil. She felt the wind against her face, whipping her hair behind her, piercing through her thin, wet clothes so that they felt like a second skin.

The storm was building up momentum. The wind now blew so strongly that the trees in its path strained at their roots. Lashing out wildly, palm fronds swerved and swooped against the sky. And still the rain quickened, pelting at the flat earth from the cloud-flattened sky.

Through the storm Jinda ran on, gulping in great mouthfuls of the wind, and feeling the rain soak her clothes to her skin. She ran until her sides hurt, until her breath came in painful gasps. And as she ran, the hard, dry knot within her began to uncoil and relax, and she felt as if a great weight were lifting from her.

The village lay far behind. Before her the rice fields stretched out, reaching to the foot of the mountains. Bathed in wet shadow, the mountains glowed a vibrant lavender.

A few farmers were already out in the field, yoking their buffaloes to start the plowing, and a few women were wading knee-deep in their seedbeds, straightening the seedlings that had been pelted into the mud.

She saw Pinit splashing in the fields, a rattan fish basket strapped across his shoulder. Together with a group of other naked boys, he stalked the little ditches now overflowing with rainwater. There might be tiny translucent shrimp for dinner tonight, and a delicate frog or two.

Pinit saw her and waved, his rib cage etched sharply under his skin. With a stab of pity, Jinda saw how thin he had grown. She waved back to him but did not feel ready to join him, or any of the exuberantly busy villagers in the fields.

Slowly she walked at the edge of the fields until she found herself near the cremation grounds. In the clearing of the grove of bodhi trees, where her father had been burned to ashes, Jinda hesitated, then walked into the grove.

It was deserted and dark under the trees, yet Jinda felt strangely drawn to the place. The thick canopy of

231

leaves sheltered her from the rain. Shadows quivered under the leaves, and she walked in gingerly, as if afraid to intrude. She felt as if she had stepped into some intensely private sphere, where the silence was a dome shielding the grove from the world outside.

She stood next to the same bodhi tree she had leaned against during the funeral as she waited for her father's coffin to burn. Jinda shut her eyes. She thought of her father and tried to remember him not as that stiff, gaunt figure lying in the coffin, nor as flakes of ash wafting through that hot afternoon. She wanted to think of him as the vibrant man who had taught her how to weave fish traps out of rattan strips, how to make a kite, how to hold a sickle. He had been tall, his eyes had crinkled at the corners when he smiled, and he had smelled of woodsmoke.

But though she remembered these details, she could not form an image of him. Jinda saw only his hand as it had cupped the clear coconut water in the coffin, the palm horribly swollen and scarred. Not that hand, Jinda thought desperately, that was not the hand that touched me and held me. His hand was strong.

And then she remembered.

His hand is big and bony, just at her eye level. His thumb is just the right size for holding onto. His fingernails are stained a reddish-brown from working in the soil, and there are hard calluses on his palm. She clings to his thumb as they cross the fields. Running along the narrow dikes, she takes two steps for every one of his, holding on to his hand for balance.

He walks fast, but steadily. He never falls. The rice stalks bow on either side of her as a breeze sifts through. Their heads of grain droop above her head. Rows and rows of brown stalks, stretching endlessly away.

"Why are they all brown?" she asks breathlessly.

"What?" His voice is dreamy, remote, far above her head.

"The stalks. Why do they turn brown? Why can't they stay fresh and green?"

"Nothing stays fresh and young forever," he says quietly. "When the stalks are young, they're green and strong. But when the rice grains form, the stalks send up all their strength to the grain, and get tired, and turn brown."

"Poor stalks," she says. "I want them to stay green."

He laughs, and his laughter stirs her like a cool breeze, making the back of her neck tingle. "But if they do, the seeds won't form, little one. And without any seeds, there won't be another rice crop the next year. The stalks have to die so that new stalks can grow after them."

"Why?"

"That is how life goes on. The old must give up their strength so the new can grow."

"Why?"

"That is just the way things are."

"But why?"

"Why, why, why!" He laughs and lifts her up, tossing her into the air. For one heart-stopping moment she is sailing above the brown fields, flying toward her father's strong, waiting arms. "Why? Because Father loves you, that's why!"

Because I love you, she echoes and laughs too.

The tears streamed down Jinda's cheeks now, merging with the rain. She wept hard, but she was laughing, too, and it was a relief to laugh and cry at the same time. Hugging the bodhi tree, her body shook so hard she had to hold on to the great tree for support.

Of course he hadn't died for an idea. Ned was wrong. Her father hadn't died for justice, or equality, or democracy. Like the strong green rice stalks that shrivel as the grain ripens, her father had given up his life for his children, so that they might grow stronger. And he had done it out of love.

Jinda wiped her cheeks and walked back into the grove. At the center of the ring of trees was the clearing, where the twin walls of brick had supported the coffin during the cremation. Mortar had crumbled in places, and a few of the bricks had fallen loose. Otherwise it was intact.

She walked up to the brick wall and rested her hands on it. There was a thin layer of black ash on the rough brick. Slowly she ran her finger across it, wiping off the thin film. Green plants to brown stalks, and a strong man to black ash.

She squatted down between the walls and scooped up a heap of ash that had accumulated there. The rain had dampened the outside layer, but deep inside the pile, the ash was still dry and loose. Carefully, Jinda brought out a handful of ash. Each flake was fragile, paper-thin.

Cupping the ash in both hands, Jinda carefully walked out into the fields. The storm was clearing, and thin streaks of light glimmered between the rain clouds. Two swallows darted out from some nearby trees, shaking tiny sprays of rain from their forked tailfeathers. In the distance, the mountains shimmered in a haze of blue.

For a moment Jinda stared at the mountains. A curtain of rain hung suspended over some of the higher peaks. Ned might be there now, feeling the rain on his skin too. Perhaps, feeling the call of the fields in the after-rain someday, he might lay down his weapons to join her again. The mountains stretched away, range beyond range, far into the distance.

A few villagers called out to her, but she avoided them, skirting the fields where people were, until she had reached her seedbed.

There it was, the patch of bright-green seedlings, quivering in the rain. Jinda stepped down from the bund into the muddy water of the seedbed. The water swirled cool and clear around her ankles. What a wonderful rain it was! Even those seedlings that had shriveled were reviving, their stems upright and taut. The sea of green stalks rippled gracefully in the wind, beautiful and alive.

"Father," Jinda said softly, and scattered her handful of ashes on each of the seedlings. The tiny black flakes drifted through the rain-fresh air and landed on the surface of the water, gathering in little clusters at the base of the seedlings.

Delicate but resilient, the young stalks glowed a tender green. If the rains continued in the next few days, all the fields could be plowed and harrowed and the seedlings at last transplanted. Choked for space now, they would thrive in the moist, muddy fields.

Jinda looked down. Already the flakes of ash were sinking into the water. Soon they would merge into the moist earth and be absorbed by the roots of the seedlings. A new crop would grow forth, nurtured by the rain and the soil and these ashes. Jinda looked up at the distant mountain range and smiled. Maybe there would be a good harvest next year after all.